Dangerous Affections

*For Sabrina and Frank, my moon
and stars, and my every breath.*

*And to 'John-John', for inspiring
me to pick up the pen.*

*With special thanks to my patient and kind editor,
James Oliveri.

<u>**CHARACTERS:**</u> *author's notes*

<u>**ELIZABETH WELLS;**</u>
Main character: 5'8", 145lbs, long dark silky hair with auburn highlights, parted on the side, light green eyes [noticeable feature], high cheek bones, large breasts. Cute, mom body, gets in shape, face nearly wrinkle free . Clothes; skinny jeans, layered sweaters, scarves, boots, leather jackets, cross body bag, well-educated, funny, sharp/cares about others-outgoing-talks to strangers easily, political organizer, relatable.
Dark side: Bored, lonely, regretful , empty-nester

<u>**PETER BALLANTYNE;**</u>
Main Character: 6'3", mid 60's, British, actor, aging but handsome, exceptionally thin, nice smile- slightly crooked, yellowed front teeth from smoking which make him look real. Direct stare- deep and sincere, salt and pepper hair -parted on the side, off and on light beard-stubble, deep smile lines, well -placed moles, long thin European nose, raspy, gravelly voice, pale, long fingers, look as though they do real work, nicks etc... intelligent and involved, sunglasses, fashion magazines, well dressed, always congenial and ever the gentleman.
Dark side: moody, controlling, desperate, maudlin

<u>**GARRETT WELLS;**</u>
Elizabeth's husband: 6 ft., 220 lbs., early 70's, asst. college football coach, HS graduate, fit, dark eyes, long eyelashes, nice-guy, easygoing, short haircuts military she hates, nice biceps, bedroom eyes. Jeans, polos, sneaks, coach clothes (black logo shorts, grey school t-shirt, sweatshirts) Large, juicy lips, crooked smile

<u>**KATHERINE WELLS;**</u>
Elizabeth and Garrett's daughter - [nickname: Kat], Tall 5'7-5'8, thin, large brown eyes, long eye lashes, long dark hair, skinny jeans, trendy tops, sneakers, beautiful skin, smart as a whip, opinionated, young, very collegiate, enthusiastic, talkative

<u>**JULIAN WELLS;**</u>
Elizabeth   and   Garrett's   son,   jock -swimmer,   studious,   pre-law   college,   girlfriend, internship, talks with mom in person/phone handsome, dark curly hair, always cut short to keep curls in check, fit, debate team, Dockers, sweaters, vests

<u>**SARAH COWEN-BALLANTYNE;**</u>
Peter's wife, mid 60's, 5'4" Blonde, curly hair, deep creases on her face, sparkling blue eyes, sour countenance as if smiling is an effort, dedicated to her kids, actress, a bit jealous of his more commercial success, once separated, rumored affairs with famous men, doting grandmother, hates country life but does ride horses, has Paris apartment, shopping, menopausal, resents he's never home...they simply co-exist

<u>**SAMANTHA BALLANTYNE;**</u>
Peter and Sarah's youngest daughter, blonde, tall, thin, light blue eyes, 'bouncy' serial dater, actress/model, insecure at times, loves 'da ddy', nice car, ultra-modern clothes, some famous friends, spoiled, school...barely graduated college

MACKENZIE BALLANTYNE;
Peter and Sarah's eldest daughter, brunette, beautiful smile, single mom, architect, serious, shoulder length hair, pretty, well-tailored clothes, baby boy always well dressed, always in a rush/busy. The more independent one, went to school at the Sorbonne

CRAZY GIRLS;

MEL
{Melanie]-Hispanic, curly black hair, crooked smile, husband Daniel, own a car repo company

LAURA
Met Elizabeth working for a non-profit, gregarious, strawberry blonde, overweight, son-does motor cross, divorced, fun, feels lonely, sleeps around nothing serious

ANNA
Owns start-up internet company, beautiful, outgoing, nice body, Elizabeth's gym partner, jock sons, husband is a successful businessman

JESSICA
Brunette, single, son has autism, youngest of the girls, always rushed, stressed, needing favors. Car always breaking down

CORRINA
Quiet, dark copper hair, a bit shy but has her moments, she had worked with Elizabeth at the United Way. Very thoughtful, always giving gifts. kind

KAREN
Blonde, muscular, large smile, incredibly sweet with a good sense of humor, always has lovely pedicures. Three kids in college

O*ne* blast in the night; neighborhood dogs barking in alarm… the deed done. Lying in a fetal position, under the warm blankets, unaware, blood pooling on the bedsheets. The figure in black turns and stealthily slips out through the glass door with a guttural whisper… "Die."

1
Chapter

Naked on the floor of her bedroom, he, sitting with his legs crossed, she, sitting in his lap; athletically, desperately, fucking each other. She orgasms as she arches her back with a twitch, he, sliding his hands down her breasts and torso as he pulls her close to him, kissing her neck.

This was the second time Elizabeth had watched this same scene of the movie tonight.

He rolled over, eyes squinting to the light generated by her computer in the darkness of their bedroom. "What time is it?" And in an accusatory voice, "What are you watching?"

Embarrassed to be caught watching a very erotic love - making scene in the movie she was streaming with 'the actor' in it, Elizabeth immediately shut her computer, took her headphones out and set them on her night table, telling Garrett, "Oh, it's nothing... just a movie," as she slid down into the bed and pulled the covers over her. "Goodnight," hoping that was the end of the questions.

She was a housewife of twenty years. Marrying at twenty-three, over time she had settled into the ebb and flow of a long-term monogamous relationship. Oh, she still loved him, deeply, and he still adored her, but they were no longer in love, and because of the age difference, with him being nearly twenty-five years her senior, the sexual part of their relationship left much to be desired .

He was still in very good shape for a man his age, with beautiful greying hair, rock hard chest, and firm calves. She still enjoyed looking at his body, but didn't desire it as she had in the past.

Still, after over twenty years together, as married people do they had evolved into a rhythm, going through life's ups and downs together, having their children, creating a history that could never be re-created with another. They had become secure in each other's company. Together they had a good life, they had a nice four-bedroom home in a good neighborhood, and the children were involved, active and very bright students.

But more and more frequently Elizabeth had been having newfound feelings of needing something more in her life. In her mid-forties now, and her sexual desire was gaining intensity as it does for many women of this age. And as she had given him her virginity, there had always been a steady curiosity of what a sexual relationship would be like with another man. They had raised their children, who had recently begun flying out of the nest and the dynamic of their lives had changed.

Elizabeth had met Garrett when she was a student at the university, he was an assistant football coach and she had been assigned to interview him for the college newspaper. New to the paper and eager to make a good impression, and though she tried to prepare for the interview, it became clear to him that she really knew nothing about football.

He thought she was charming acting businesslike and serious so he helped her out by both asking and answering questions for her.

"You know you should come to the game on Saturday and learn about it, I can leave you a ticket at Will Call. You can sit near the bench," he smiled.

The article on him came out the next day and painted a good picture.

She hadn't really given the coach another thought, until one day a week later he called the paper and said he wanted to thank her for writing such a nice article .

"Elizabeth, hi it's Garrett Wells-Coach Wells"

"Hi, Coach. What's up?" Surprised by the call.

"I read the interview article, it was really great, thank you."

She thought he sounded upbeat and genuinely happy about it.

"But I want to say thank you properly for making me look so good. Will you let me take you to dinner tomorrow night?"

She was surprised by the invitation, but she had been so wrapped up with studying lately, the thought of a night out was exciting.

"Sure, that sounds fun." Genuinely liking his personality, she thought it would be nice to get to know him.

The next evening, as she waited with excitement and anxiety for him to pick her up at her apartment, checking and rechecking her makeup and her outfit in the mirror, not sure if her clothes were too young, or her dress too short, she was nervous. Basically, he was a stranger aside from their interview, and she was worried she wouldn't know what to talk about.

He opened the car door for her before they drove to the restaurant. Waiting for him to get in, she thought, guys my age don't do that. It was nice.

The coach was only a few years younger than Elizabeth's parents, so as they walked into the restaurant together, his hand on her back, she felt like everyone was staring at them. She felt the burn rise in her cheeks with this thought. He helped her off with her coat, another gentlemanly gesture she noted.

Once they were seated they talked easily, and both had good senses of humor. He asked, "Have you ever noticed how Prof. Strand walks across campus?" Smiling he went on, "He's so hunched over he looks really uncomfortable. The team calls him a carpet inspector!"

She snorted at the comment. He was goofy sometimes, but he was growing on her.

By the end of their third date she was smitten, but feared what her mother might think. This time they went to a movie, a comedy where they both laughed out loud and shared popcorn. Neither ever said anything about the age difference. They were just two people who enjoyed each other's company, and the feeling she had about people looking at them eventually began to wear off.

At the end of the date, Garrett leaned over and asked, "May I kiss you?"

Elizabeth thought that was the sweetest thing she'd ever heard. No guy had ever asked her permission. Feeling nervous and a bit insecure, but she was attracted to him, and besides, she didn't think she could resist his big, kissable, juicy lips.

"You may," she nodded her consent . As it turned out he was a terrific kisser.

She accompanied him to an away game a few weeks later. They boarded the buses just past daybreak Friday morning outside the athletic building. Wth a chill still in the air, she felt second thoughts creeping up, about being on the bus with the players, but her desire to spend more time with him won out.

The team won that afternoon and were on a winning streak. After the game, leaning against a cement wall that looked as though it had been painted over with a dull, white paint several times and smelled of mildew and old gym socks, she waited around for the players and the coach to shower -up, wondering what the night had in store.

Garrett came out freshly washed and smelling of soap, hair still a bit damp, "Are you hungry?" he wanted to know.

"Starved. I only had a hotdog and that was hours ago." Elizabeth smiled.

Garrett took her to a quiet dinner at a restaurant near the hotel. They talked over plates of spaghetti and meatballs, she, trying desperately to twirl the strands on her fork and eat it without getting it all over her mouth like she would at home.

She noticed as usual he seemed genuinely interested in what she had to say, and she had discovered over the weeks that he was a great guy, a gentleman, and that he had apparently fallen for her.

"Coach…" she said.

"I told you, please call me Garrett."

"Sorry, Garrett. Can I ask you a personal question?"

Smiling, he said, "Sure, if I retain the right to not answer if I don't want to."

She smiled, too. "Have you ever been married?"

He thought for a moment, fingering the discarded paper from his straw. "I almost was once," he explained, "but the timing wasn't right. I was really into getting my career rolling, she had been offered a position as an attorney back east, and I had just gotten my first promotion at the university. It just didn't work out."

Elizabeth pressed, "Do you have any regrets?"

Shaking his head slightly, he said, "No just that I'm getting older and I thought I would have kids by now."

"How many do you want?"

"I'd like maybe two or three," he smiled. "How about you, are kids in your future?"

She replied, "Wow, I haven't given it a lot of thought, I feel like a kid myself sometimes. Right now, I'm just worried about passing European Political Theory!"

Garrett had thought of everything for the weekend including getting her a room of her own at the hotel, and as she sat back on the chaise lounge in her room, reflecting on their day and night, fighting the butterflies in her stomach, with a smile she couldn't quite wipe off her face, she rang his room.

"Hi, Garrett. I'm having trouble with something. Could I get your help?"

"Sure, no problem." He said he could be there in a few minutes.

She had already decided this was the man she wanted to give her virginity to. She was ready now and he was kind and caring. When she was younger other guys tried, but with all their fumbling, and her seeing right through them, that it wasn't about her, it was about them, she never felt that anyone truly cared enough. The coach made her feel different.

When he knocked on the door she bit her lip. She was nervous but sure of her decision. As he stepped into the room, she shut the door behind him. He turned to face her and she put her arms around him and asked him to kiss her.

He asked, "Are you sure, Elizabeth?"

She felt herself blush, but smiled and said, "Yeah, I'm sure."

They made love that night, he knowing he was her first, was gentle and slow and very romantic. "Am I hurting you? Tell me and I'll stop."

"No, it's OK… I can handle it."

He eventually gave her an orgasm with him inside her, and she felt like she finally knew what all the fuss was about.

A few short weeks later, he told her he loved her. She told him she couldn't tell him something she wasn't feeling yet. She hated to give such a disappointing answer, but felt it was still early in their relationship, and she had always been cautious, so they continued to go on dates, making out in his car, but it was only a short two weeks later with him being in her every thought that she told him that she indeed was in love with him, too.

After graduation, they got married in a tiny chapel in Las Vegas, with a small cadre of family and friends. And after four years of marriage, their son Julian was born, a future ' hall of famer' in the making, but it wasn't until their daughter Kat was born two years later that Elizabeth saw real love in his eyes. She would forever be daddy's little girl.

He had always tried hard to be at the kids' sport practices, games, recitals, and pageants, beaming and bringing flowers. He was a good father to his children; he felt proud of them.

In addition to having his own son to teach and advise, he had always loved working with his players. The boys he had worked with over the years had always been special to him, like sons in a way.

Many had issues at home, or were dirt poor or never had fathers in their lives. He was involved with the head coach in recruiting new players, and over the years he had met some fine young men, football players, boys in need. It gave him a great deal of pleasure when he could utter, "Son, we would love to have you come play ball for us at the university."

Garrett was such an easygoing guy and with a caring spirit they could feel, the boys always took to him right away. The eager boys wanted to know, "Will I be working out with you coach?"

It was hard not to take them all but when the new - recruit classes arrived every year he always loved watching their wonderment and the change in their circumstances. They realized they were somebody and that they had worth and were important. The transformation was almost magical. But this brought with it Garrett's need to protect them from over - exposure and helping to develop their character so that they were not just football players, they were young gentleman, not full of themselves but eager to be of service, humble, at least that was the goal he had for his players.

2

Chapter

He turned seventy-two this past August. He had given her and the children a good, stable, and loving life, if only lacking a bit in the excitement department. And it was this... excitement, which was exactly what Elizabeth felt was missing from her life now.

She felt herself growing older, and an increasing feeling of urgency to do something more with her life, to take the road less traveled, at least throughout her life thus far. She was well - educated and always curious about a great many things. She'd spend hours on the internet looking up just about everything imaginable and the time was always well-spent. At one time when she was younger she had considered going to law school and now she was missing a challenge like that. The rest had become routine. She needed more. She wasn't sure what that was yet, but she knew she needed more.

Over their many years together she'd had a few serious temptations with other men, a co-worker from a previous job. They had begun to fall for each other after working on a series of projects requiring long hours at work together, alone, eating meals together, and bouncing ideas off one another.

There was her sister's father-in-law whom she had feelings for long before turning eighteen, and while the feelings were mutual it was never discussed or acted upon until she was older. He was desperately trying to seduce her. A few men drew her in more than they should have over the years, but nevertheless she would always put on the brakes before anything could ever really happen, citing always the love of her husband and the strong desire not to hurt him.

So, what had changed as of late? She still loved her husband and desired not to hurt him, the same as always. She often sat alone in her kitchen, wondering what it was that she needed at this point in her life to make her feel fulfilled.

She had begun feeling her own mortality, and a bit of regret for always doing things for others, and having buried that spark of her youth for new experiences, desire for travel, sexual excitement, in a sense, her freedom.

When she looked at herself in the mirror, her body had changed over the years, now resembling a more "Mom" type body than a sexy co-ed, but still the desire to look and feel good was there. As she applied her makeup she was always happy to see that she was aging nicely, without any real wrinkles to speak of yet. "You still got it girl" she would tell herself. She had always had nice, plump breasts, but was struggling always to firm up and enlarge her rear-end...she wore her hair straight, a bit below her shoulders, brown with a touch of auburn.

"OK, Rita, I want to throw in a hint of red, or auburn to the dark brown, liven it up a bit, what do you think?"

"I think it will look awesome, Elizabeth, fresh and healthy". Her stylist of many years, Rita always had a way of making her feel that her every suggestion was just tops.

In the end, the color enhanced and brought out her already uniquely beautiful green eyes. And as clothes shopping was her secret addiction she usually had the latest fashion trends for her age group with a little younger flair thrown in for fun. She loved boots, and jeans and unique jackets and coats, in greens and browns.

After graduating from college, she had gravitated toward work as a fundraiser in the non -profit industry, spending over fifteen years in the industry. There was opportunity to meet many influential people, including handsome, wealthy men. But she wouldn't regret settling so young for another decade or so.

From modest means never really desiring immense wealth, more happily surrounded by family and her friends, including her group of 'crazy girls', the wine-drinking, wise-cracking group of fellow moms who got together once or twice a month for a night of laughter and friendship .

Most of them were now empty-nesters also, and had raised their kids well and had sent them off to colleges around the country.

Elizabeth's kids studied hard and both got into the colleges of their choices. Kat was so happy the day she came running in from the mail box. "Mommy, Mommy guess what? I got in, I got in. Vassar wants me…Ahhhh!" She screamed.

Julian had been accepted to Columbia two years earlier. Elizabeth told her husband in exasperation, "These kids went just about as far away from Los Angeles, and us, as they could ," as they had both fled from L.A. to New York.

The crazy girls had much in common and similar stories to share and commiserate with one another as they adjusted to life without the kids. Many of the women expressed desires for the next chapter of their lives, including returning to school, or travel, and even a few planning on having an affair. Elizabeth now wondered if this was an option she should exercise.

What had changed that even had her contemplating something so far flung, she didn't know. Elizabeth always listened with interest as they described what they all wanted for their futures. She never volunteered much about her plans or thoughts because she really hadn't thought much about what was next for her, until recently.

3
Chapter

It all started innocently enough. She began watching Netflix movies on her computer with headphones at night with her husband sleeping soundly and snoring next to her. She had always been jealous of his being able to fall asleep quickly and into a deep sleep. She thought, 'a woman seems to lose this ability as soon as she becomes a mom, instinctively.' So, she gave up trying to match his schedule now, and would stay up into the early morning watching movies she had always told herself she would see when she had time.

She began re-watching movies she had seen and loved, movies that took her back to her childhood, "The Bad News Bears," and the teenage years, Tom Cruise in "Risky Business ," remembering now the huge crush she had on him then. She even took a spell at taking in old movies, and movies that mattered, one of her favorites, "Look Who's Coming to Dinner," Sydney Poitier, Katherine Hepburn, and her favorite, Spencer Tracy, to a couple of cowboy classics, "Who Shot Liberty Valance" and the like.

Every now and then, she would watch different movies starring a movie star, Peter Ballantyne, who had been around a while. He was British, tall, and handsome. He was a good actor, and renowned for it. She always thought him very handsome and European, so European that she at one point even thought he might be gay. Still, she enjoyed the movies that she watched with him in them, without giving another thought about him. *Until she did.*

After watching a psychological thriller one night in which she thought he looked and sounded very sexy, the next night she found herself searching Netflix for other films that he had been in, and there were many to choose from.

When she watched another of his movies, a great film by an Italian director with a series of fantastic over -the-top love scenes, s*he really took notice this time.*

The love-making scenes in the movie were so racy she was surprised that it only had an "R" rating. It was quite good, so good in fact it had awakened her to feelings of wanting raw sex that she hadn't had in a while, as well as the desire for romance and intimacy which was missing in her relationship with Garrett.

She realized she needed to be touched, by a new man, experiencing the thrill and excitement of engaging in long, lingering, romantic kisses. She wanted an orgasm at the end of hot and frantic passion, she knew now that she wanted what she was seeing in this movie. She missed it, she needed it.

Replaying some of the naughtier parts to see them again, hoping her husband sleeping next to her wouldn't wake and think that she spent her awake time watching sex movies.

The following day as she went about her business, not giving a returning thought to the actor so much as the depth to which the movie had moved her, and the feelings it had stirred. She'd had these thoughts before but she could usually bury them, accept her lot in life and soldier on. "Come on Elizabeth, you are just sad about the kids being gone. Snap out of it," she would say out loud as if those magic words would fix everything.

That evening when she watched another movie, she intentionally chose one that Ballantyne was not in. She did this for a few nights, in an attempt, to divert her attention from him and to try and shake the feelings about him, of being physically attracted to him, which were gaining in intensity with each new movie. She loved his handsome face, the etched lines that were proof that he lived a full and exciting life.

She would study his hands, the long, slim fingers. She began to fantasize about them. She wanted him to touch her. She wanted those hands on her body.

As she did her house cleaning and errands during her days her mind would began drifting back to 'him', Peter Ballantyne, the actor she watched pretending to make love on screen. She began to wonder, was it the movie scenes that had captured her fancy or was it him specifically?

That evening she couldn't resist, she wathced yet another movie starring the actor, an American Western in which he couldn't quite lose his English accent, which she found charming. He had a long line of movies to his credit. He was a bona-fide movie star.

As she watched, she began to think that, yes, maybe it was the man regardless of the role he was playing that she found herself so attracted to.

She could picture him, Peter Ballantyne making love to her, kissing her, talking softly to her. When he was younger she had thought him a great actor and nothing more. Now with his aging gracefully, and no doubt she always found older men attractive, he suddenly looked very enticing to her. "Why the hell is this guy in my head?" she wondered. "He is a movie star-untouchable. I'm acting like a teenager with a crush on her teacher."

Over the next few week she watched additional movies he was in, as a military leader, or a doctor, mythical creatures, constantly keeping her on a slow simmer. By now she was convinced she was smitten with him, and with the advent of greater technology, she began looking him up on the internet, feeling halfway like a teenager, and a stalker, but it was fun to do.

Then she accessed the Holy Grail -his website. She knew it was managed by his 'handlers', but it provided news on things he had done, was doing, and would be doing, 'Peter Ballantyne to appear on an Italian talk show.' 'Peter Ballantyne has been cast in a new picture opening early next year', the site also had a plethora of information about his life in general.

She discovered he was married to an actress, and for many years, a tough gig for anyone in Hollywood. But Elizabeth was happy for him. It told of his two daughters who were now grown and into their adult lives. His career seemed to be at full speed again after a few slow years, which she assumed meant he now spent less time at home and numerous days on movie sets and theater stages.

At this point, Elizabeth found herself thinking about him daily, and she relished keeping her little secret to herself.

The more 'research' she did on him she found him to be highly intelligent, a thoughtful speaker and a kind man. 'Peter Ballantyne joins campaign to stop animal abuse.' 'Actor supports prison poetry project that helps inmates express themselves through writing.'

'Academy Award Winning Actor to help raise money for Autism research', were some of the headlines with his name attached. To Elizabeth it meant that he was a thinker, he had a brain and used it, not like many of the actors around today who were simply publicity hounds and overly concerned with Twitter followers.

Having married a man with only a high school education, and Elizabeth being educated at a top notch renowned university, she often missed high caliber discussions and debate with highly intelligent minds. She could tell that this man, who was twenty years her senior, was very articulate and thought provoking. His comments to interview questions and appearances had made her begin to debate his topics within her mind. Although he was considered controversial in some of his thinking, this never interfered with his acting career and the fans who loved him.

She relished poring over the hundreds of photos and videos on Ballantyne's website, and through this she finally became convinced that she had to meet him. She had a genuine desire to talk to him, engage him in conversation. He appeared to be a good conversationalist and listener with a terrific sense of humor and he seemed like someone she would really like to know, regardless of her other feelings.

Although she admitted to herself a meeting was far - fetched, and nearly impossible, as he was a movie star, a very famous one, and very wealthy, she knew meeting him would not be easy. But she was a smart girl. She'd think of something . This finally convinced her that she was indeed ready, in fact, overdue for an adventure, and maybe he was it.

As she contemplated her first move she became excited. She decided this was the time she and Kat had been waiting for. They would finally execute the trip they had talked about for over a year. Their first trip to Europe. They had spent the last year or more daydreaming and planning this great trip. They both had many similar interests in what they wanted to see and do. Elizabeth felt that her daughter had grown into her young adulthood and that she was losing a bit of her, and thought that this trip would be a tremendous bonding, learning experience and one that Kat could carry with her all her life . It didn't hurt matters that Ballantyne lived in Europe.

After talking it over on the phone with Kat, still away at school, and with much excitement, they began making lists of "to dos" in preparation.

They had to start by arranging for online classes and independent study through Kat's school so she wouldn't fall behind during their trip. The trip, a sort of backpacking through Europe adventure, was to last three to four months. It would be the trip of a lifetime, and Elizabeth could think of no one she'd rather spend it with than her daughter.

4
Chapter

Their plan would include trips to England, Ireland, France, Italy, Germany, and all the great places between, big cities and little towns. They started the preparations by applying for their passports. Neither of them had been out of America, except a few quick trips to Baja, Mexico, which hadn't required one, and although her daughter had contemplated doing a school semester abroad, she eventually decided against it because of a certain boy at the time.

When Kat came home for long weekends or holidays, they sat down and mapped out their journey, filling in dates of must-sees and dos.

"Mom, can we please, please go to the 'running of the bulls' in Pamplona?" Kat's eyes implored her.

"Yes-to watch! Oh, and let's do the 'Tomatina', the tomato throwing festival, also in Spain," Elizabeth added.

They included all the important dates throughout Europe, a regatta in Italy, Cannes, France during the film festival.

"I've heard that anyone who is a famous actor goes to that film festival. I wonder who we'll see?" Kat mused.

They were very excited as they began scouting sporting goods stores looking for the best backpacks, and good, cute walking boots. The realization that this was finally happening had them overjoyed.

Elizabeth had always been a good writer, convinced this was how she made it through college. So, she decided she was going to propose ghost writing Ballantyne's autobiography, his memoirs.

In her 'research' of him she had found no biography, only magazine articles and interviews. But she decided that to be successful she would not go about asking him in the 'usual' way. She thought her best chance was to do it her own way, not through his managers. No publicists, too many people to say 'no' before he even would see the proposal, she thought, and without other writing credentials she feared she would be seen as an amateur and not be taken seriously by them. Her idea was instead to find a way to meet him face to face. So, as their plans for the trip began to take shape, Elizabeth began to work on this new twist in hopes it would all come together.

According to his website, the actor would be receiving an honor at a film festival in Prague during their time in Europe. The festival was open to the public, and tickets were being sold online for the movie screenings and award galas, etc.

Elizabeth bought the full festival passes for herself and her daughter. They would at least be in the same room as he was. That was exciting enough, but she would look for any opportunity to speak with him one on one about the proposal. At least that was the goal.

By this time, Kat had also become aware of the 'slight' crush her mom had on this actor. She thought it would pass and didn't give it another thought. But even she became excited when her mother filled her in on her intentions of meeting him in Prague.

"I am going to submit a proposal to him to write his biography," and as he was going to be in a movie Kat had been waiting for nearly a year to come out, the thought that they might actually meet him was exciting for her, too.

Garrett had been aware of the intention for the two of them to take this kind of trip and initially he considered going with them. Instead he had booked a trip for himself to visit his relatives in Northern Canada, two months before football spring training camp would begin, while their son Julian completed his senior year in college before starting his summer internship and law school next fall.

That was the family plan. Also, Garrett knew this would be a great experience for the two of them, on their own, discovering more about one another. A real mother -daughter thing. Elizabeth did not fill him in on her intentions regarding the proposal to Ballantyne, so of course Garrett never had reason to expect anything other than the girls vacationing in Europe, and he was excited for them.

Part of physically planning for a meeting with Ballantyne included Elizabeth developing a professional proposal asking the actor if she could write his memoirs and creating rationale for her asking as well as his agreeing to it.

She made it easy for him, saying she would accommodate his schedule, meet him where she needed to. She included a mock-up of a potential book cover, front and back, with a selection of pictures, as well as a list of possible subjects his fans would like to know about. The presentation was very professional, but with a little of her humor thrown in for flavor.

There were many little details to complete it to her liking. She would use professional linen stationery, making sure he had multiple ways of contacting her, as well as an explanation as to why she didn't want to go through 'proper' channels to ask him. Once she felt it was complete, she sealed it in a large envelope, putting it safely in her new backpack.

As they counted down the time for their trip to begin, Elizabeth helped her husband prepare for his trip, buying some new clothes and toiletries. "What do you think about this? You always look so good in brown," she said, holding up a plump sweater.

"Really honey, I don't think I need all this stuff," Garrett said in exhaustion. The mall was very busy as usual. He had his fill of shopping for the day, he really just wanted to go home, lie on the sofa, and catch the game. His flight would be leaving the same day as Elizabeth's, but later in the day. She was going to miss him and he her, but each felt in their own way that some time apart could be good for them.

But Elizabeth was now holding a bit of guilt in her heart because she knew an additional reason for this trip that she hadn't shared with him.

"Why don't I tell him? I'm not doing anything wrong, I'm asking him to write his memoirs." But deep down she knew that the feelings the actor had stirred in her were wrong and the thrill it gave her she wanted to keep for herself.

Los Angeles International Airport was busy as usual, especially the Bradley International Flights Terminal, honking horns, taxis rushing by, shuttles making their circuits, which was annoying to Elizabeth after already spending over an hour in Los Angeles traffic.

Because airports do not let non-ticketed passengers accompany travelers to the gates anymore, and their flights were hours apart, they had to say their goodbyes before entering the security checkpoint.

Elizabeth and Garrett hugged for a long time, finally he said, "Please be careful. With all this stuff going on in the world, it's kind of scary."

She responded "You be careful, too. Canada isn't as far away from home, but things can happen. I'll miss you and I love you," she said.

Squeezing her tighter, he said, "I love you too, babe. You'd better get going. You don't want to miss your flight." Kat and he had already said their goodbyes ending with a fist bump.

As she and Kat checked their backpacks and made their way to their gate, they both became giggly and excited, the kind of jubilation you get when being let out of school before a holiday.

"Mom, I'm so stoked for this trip." Smiling Kat was genuinely excited, and Elizabeth loved to see that. Kat had been known to struggle with bouts of maudlin over the years, so to see her in such a good and optimistic mood made Elizabeth's heart smile.

After waiting in the terminal for about an hour and a half, sipping their Starbucks and people watching, they both had a terrible habit of making fun of people amongst themselves, something Elizabeth felt bad about letting her daughter get away with, but they were both very clever and had good senses of humor, so it was kind of their 'thing'. They were finally allowed to board the plane. They would be flying British Airways into their first stop, Dublin, Ireland on the day before St. Patrick's Day.

Being of Irish heritage, this was one stop Elizabeth insisted they make.

5
Chapter

Ireland would be a twelve-and-a half hour flight that they hoped would go fast, between watching movies, listening to music, sleeping, and their meals. Upon boarding they immediately noticed the flight crew speaking the Queen's English, a sure sign that their adventure had begun.

They enjoyed flying over snowcapped mountains, large bodies of water, high above the clouds. They would feel cabin temperatures change with the scenery, Elizabeth noting that her behind began to get sore the last two hours or so. And while Kat slept, passed out on Elizabeth's shoulder, she could smell the shampoo in Kat's hair, a smell that she remembered from when Kat was little. The thought made her smile.

They landed at night in the freezing cold, waiting outside for the shuttle bus to their hotel.

"Mom, we have been out here for over an hour, I can't feel my face. Where is our shuttle?"

They had watched numerous shuttles come around again and again, but none with the logo of their hotel on it. Elizabeth finally rechecked with the shuttle stop attendant as to which shuttle they were waiting for.

"It's the purple one, lass", he told her. As she walked back to Kat, she thought, the unmarked purple one that had already made two passes? They were nearly frozen solid on its third pass, until they hopped on, finally headed for their hotel which was nothing special, a typical Howard Johnson's.

They had an early wake up call, wanting to get an early start, to get down to O'Connell Street early for a good view of the parade.

Of course, they had to stop in a store or two to get their St. Patrick's Day attire, beads, hats etc., and a warm cup of Starbucks. Although Elizabeth felt excited she also felt a bit out of place, this was their first stop in Europe.

The store clerk asked her for "eight pounds, forty-five pence" for her purchase. Elizabeth looking at the bills and coins the money exchange people had given her at the airport and trying to do the math finally she just held out her hand, blushing, so the clerk could take the correct amount. This was going to take some getting used to.

"Wow, Mom, look at all these people!"

There were people as far as the eye could see in all directions. The parade goers had a good camaraderie, and everyone was having a good time, discovering they had come from far and wide for this day.

As the floats went by, Elizabeth and Kat realized that the parade they had expected was far different from what they were seeing. In the United States, St. Patrick's Day parades were about leprechauns, beads, Irish bands, but in Dublin, the floats were all very Art Deco and modern sculptures, some crazy designs, others completely abstract. While it was fun, it wasn't exactly what they thought they were in for. They took plenty of photos and selfies for memories.

After the parade, every person on O'Connell street headed into the handful of pubs nearby, including Kat and Elizabeth. They went into Madigan's, already filled to the gills, with patrons. They were serving up hearty dishes of Irish stews and corned beef and cabbage, and of course pulling frothy ice-cold Guinness. The girls found a seat at a table with other friendly souls, Marta and Louisa, whom they discovered were visiting from Spain. The girls then partook in the authentic food and drink.

At one point, Kat announced, "Mom, I really need to use the restroom, where do you think it is?" Looking around, Elizabeth spotted a sign with an arrow, and motioned to Kat. She excused herself, and weaved between the many patrons on her way.

It had been a good fifteen minutes that Kat was gone. Elizabeth originally thought it was because with that many patrons, the ladies' room was always the busiest. But after a few more minutes, she became concerned. She then weaved her way to the bathroom as well and she walked right in. No line at all.

She could see there were women in the stalls, so she whispered, "Kat?"

"Oh Mom, thank God." Kat sounded relieved.

"What is it, honey?" said Elizabeth, concerned. Trying to stay calm and not embarrass herself, Kat said,

"Mom- I'm stuck in this stall!"

In this particular bathroom, these particular stalls extended nearly the entire height of the wall. There was no room to either crawl out the bottom or climb over the top. With a bit of a laugh, Elizabeth said, "Are you serious?"

"Yes, Mom, it's not funny." Kat said with attitude.

"Actually Kat, it is kinda funny. Let me get someone, hang in there."

On the busiest day of the year for this pub, she had to pull a bartender, or server, not sure which, away from his job to rescue her daughter. He was delightful and charming, acting as though it was no problem at all. He came from behind the bar area and she followed him to the ladies' room. He announced, "Ladies, if you are in a stall, please stay in there. There is a man in here, performing a bit of a rescue."

The guy, short and stocky, reminded Elizabeth of exactly what you'd think an Irish boxer looked like, and with a thick Irish brogue. He stood on the adjoining toilet and peeked over to Kat through the little space available at the top.

"No worries, love. I'll have you out in a jiffy, just stand back from the door." He then came around to the front of the door, and just like a bull or a super hero, took a running start, crashing into the stall door, which did not open! Rubbing his shoulder, he muttered "Let me try that again." The second blast against the door worked, sending the door's hardware sputtering to the ground. "See love, no problem."

He offered his hand to Kat, who looked relieved.

"Thank you so much."

"Oh no, lass, no problem. Come on down and have a pint on the house."

After touring the city's landmarks and a bit of shopping, they headed back to the hotel for a good night's sleep. They had fulfilled that bucket list item, but their stay in Ireland was to be short.

The next morning, they boarded a 'ferry', a rather large ship, to cross from the Emerald Isle to Wales. They had six days before the film festival in Prague was to start.

Their plan was a brief stop in England, then on to Italy for a few days. They were anxious to see it all, even though they knew they had plenty of time and would be revisiting these places, but they were excited and anxious to see and to do.

They arrived from their ferry trip in Wales, and decided to take a train directly to London and spent only the night in London, as their ultimate place to start their journey was Italy. In the morning, they boarded a small jet that would whisk them to Rome. During the taxi ride from the airport in Rome to their hotel they struggled to understand the strong Italian accent of their driver, who after having to repeat what he was saying three times, basically shouted the fourth time, pointing to the "Vaticano-Il Papa - The Pope!"

Oh my gosh, right outside their window lay before them the Vatican City, the Vatican, glorious, as they zoomed by. They would be returning by foot the next day.

Sipping their morning Cappuccino in the hotel's little café, "This is so exciting isn't it Mom? We have so much to see today and I am so ready for this."

They were both very excited about the day's agenda; first up-the Vatican. They would tour St. Peters Basilica, where it is said the actual tomb of St. Peter, the apostle appointed by Jesus to lead the Christian faith lies. They also toured the Borgia Apartments, named after Pope Alexander VI who had them remodeled and which now served as the Cardinals' residences. As well as the Apostolic Palace, where the current Pope actually resides.

With their tourist headphones on, they toured the Vatican Museum. They marveled at the Sistine Chapel where visitors are encouraged to lie on leather sofas to view the glorious frescos of Michelangelo's 'The Last Judgement,' and 'The Creation of Adam'.

Elizabeth, in an awed whisper to Kat, "This is breathtaking. Remember this Kat, this is special, sacred."

There were many other works of exquisite art, Renaissance works by Raphael, the Gallery of the Candelabra, home to carved marble candelabras and sculptures and the Gallery of Maps, where they saw dozens of intricate maps of Italy from the sixteenth century. There were other works including Egyptian and Greek as well.

While they were there they also put their names on a list to be chosen for getting tickets to the Papal Easter Mass in the square, as they would still be in Europe at Easter time. Having an audience with the Pope would be the ultimate in their journey.

"You know Kat, my ancestors were very Catholic, and I am a bad Catholic as I am not practicing and hardly ever attend church, but seeing the Pope would mean so much to me and would have meant the world to my grandparents who never had the chance."

Their day had already been so full, but they wanted to see more. They toured the Forum and its ruins on a grand scale, viewing the juxtaposition of the buildings, monuments, aqueducts, and the planning that went into the ancient city.

They visited the Colosseum, with Kat asking Elizabeth if she too felt the presence of all the audiences, and the terror that the gladiators must have felt when facing the most ferocious beasts. Elizabeth told her she did indeed.

Their day ended in a local sidewalk pizza café as the sun was going down. Tomorrow, would be another busy day, so after dinner they fell into bed for the night, exhausted.

Waking in a beautiful Italian city felt like heaven on earth. The sun shone differently, the smells were different, the people loud and vibrant. They spent the early part of the day in the square poking into little shoe shops, little boutique clothing shops with local and Milanese fashions. Of course, there were plenty of souvenir shops with post cards, magnets, coffee mugs and the like. Later that evening they would be taking a train to the city of Lucca.

Leaving Rome, the train was virtually empty. New to the whole train thing, Elizabeth approached the one person in their car with them. She was youngish and pretty, Italian. Elizabeth asked her if there were taxi stands at each of the train stops so they could get to their hotel from the train.

As they talked, the girl, Yvetta, asked if they were from the U.S. They got caught up in talking, and when the train stopped, the doors did not open automatically. They had learned, too late, that on some trains you have to physically push the button and as they talked they didn't realize the door hadn't opened, the train began its forward journey again. That prompted Yvetta to shout "No!" and hit the window. Too late. The train was at a full roll now. Yvetta left her bags and took off running through the adjoining cars toward the front of the train.

After Yvetta being gone a few minutes Kat spoke up. "Mom, what are we going to do? The next stop is the end of the line."

"Well, I guess we are sleeping on the train," thinking this the only way to keep them safe.

Finally, Yvetta came back. "The conductor said he can't stop. It's too late."

Elizabeth spoke up now feeling bad that this happened because she had distracted Yvetta, but also a bit scared. "I am so sorry."

"Not to worry. Well, the next stop is thirty miles past Lucca."

"Wow, thirty miles," Elizabeth said shocked.

"Yes, it's the last stop." Yvetta informed her.

"Oh My God, I am so sorry," Elizabeth feeling anxious and embarrassed.

Yvetta was kind. "Non, no. It was my fault." Taking them under her care she said, "We'll get off at the next stop, and talk to a taxi driver." Now feeling in her debt, they readily agreed.

At the stop both women reached for the button to open the door at the same time, laughing. The three got out in a hurry. Yvetta took charge and knew where the taxi stand was, as she was from Lucca, so she knew her way around this area. As she stooped to talk to the first taxi driver, her voice rose, and she threw her hands up, walking away in disgust. Elizabeth asked, "What happened?"

"The crazy, he wants €70 to take us to Lucca." Shaking her head.

"Wow, €70. Let me ask the second driver." Elizabeth suggested a kind of a 'no-no' anywhere, but they were desperate. The second driver told Elizabeth also €70, so she walked back to Yvetta and Kat. She said, "Well I have fifty Euro on me. Do you have twenty?"

"No...No, that is crazy prices. No way. Listen," she said. "I call my friends, they will give us ride to Lucca."

Elizabeth, feeling more embarrassed, said, "Oh no, I couldn't ask them to do that."

"No-no, really, it's fine," Yvetta reassured. "It'll be good. They are really nice, yes?"

Elizabeth shot a look of uncertainty to Kat, thinking that Yvetta seemed nice enough, not a weirdo and, really, they were out of options. "Sure, OK." She looked at Kat and shrugged her shoulders.

As they waited the twenty minutes for her friends to arrive, there was a little bar on the breezeway that was still open, so they stepped in and ordered three white wine spritzers, cheered each other, for their predicament, and to meeting new people.

They made casual conversation with the two elderly Italian bartenders, who asked about their travel plans, and about America.

When Yvetta's friends arrived, they jumped out of their car, a very small black Fiat. They hugged Yvetta as she had just returned from a week away on vacation, then they came to Kat and Elizabeth and hugged them, too, saying they were sorry for their problems, and they would be happy to take them to Lucca. After five people and four large backpacks were crammed into the little car, it was on. The driver, a handsome young Italian named Luigi, drove like he was on the German Autobahn, fast-very fast, taking corners and curves like Mario Andretti.

Kat and Elizabeth shot each other nervous looks. Nicoletta, the girlfriend, asked Elizabeth where in Lucca they were staying. Elizabeth told her the name of the Bed & Breakfast.

"Oh yes, I know this one. We will take you there."

"You are really too kind. Thank you so much," Elizabeth said truly grateful.

"No problem. We like Americans," she laughed.

As they pulled into a side street, Elizabeth saw the sign of the B&B, and that the lobby appeared to be closed.

She realized their delay had put them past lobby hours.

Could this night get any more complicated? She thought. She did have a phone number which she dialed.

The owner of the B&B didn't live onsite. He began to tell Elizabeth, "No, you come too late. We have left for the night."

As Elizabeth began to explain why they were late, Yvetta gestured to give her the phone. When she got on she rattled off in Italian with a bit of attitude, basically telling him the story and why he had to come back and check them in.

"OK, OK, ciao," she said. Smiling to Elizabeth, "Giovanni is on his way."

They all laughed and it became jovial small talk and from then on, every car that passed the Italians' would say, "Giovanni?"

"No Giovanni," to the next car, "Giovanni? No, no Giovanni."

It left the girls laughing and feeling safer. Finally, a car pulled up out front, out came Giovanni.

"Giovanni?"

"Si...Si."

"Ah Giovanni, grazie, grazie," the Italians went on, the Italian girls hugging him.

Giovanni said to Elizabeth, "I didn't know you had friends in Lucca," smiling to Yvetta and Nicoletta.

"I do now," Elizabeth smiled.

Luigi helped the girls get their luggage into the small hotel, and after there were hugs all around, Yvetta and Elizabeth exchanged phone numbers with a promise to have lunch.

The Italians left, and Giovanni was charming and led the girls to their room. The girls were exhausted. It didn't take long for them to hit the beds and pass out until morning. Did they treat every day as a celebration? She could get used to their people very easily, Elizabeth thought as she drifted off.

Over espresso in the morning Kat and Elizabeth relived their night, and couldn't believe how nice and friendly the Italians were to them, or that they had actually taken the slightly dangerous option.

"Luigi was sooo cute, but he drove like a bat out of Hell," Kat said, recalling the experience.

"I'm just glad we made it in one piece," said Elizabeth with a smirk.

6
Chapter

Lucca was unique. It is one of the still standing walled cities of ancient Italy. They learned it was built as such to keep enemies out, the entire city is inside the wall, and although the architecture is ancient and authentic, the squares now held fashion shops, gelato stores, and all the modern conveniences.

There were numerous churches, theaters, but as the architecture was original, it gave the feeling of still being small and old world. No heavy advertising in the shops. People lived and worked here. There still stood many old apartment buildings with balconies and window boxes full of flowers. The streets were small and many were cobblestone. It was as if she and Kat were transported back to another time. They visited the square that housed the childhood home of Puccini, the composer of La Boehm and Madame Butterfly, still standing as it was during the time he lived there.

Climbing atop the wall was still allowed, intended for visitors to survey the entire city, with its red-tiled roofs and spires and duomos.

They were transfixed by the city. They had learned from their tour guides that in 56 BC the Lucca Conference, considered the 'first triumvirate', had taken place here, attended by Julius Caesar, Pompey, and Crassus. Also, that the writer Dante had spent some years in exile here, and after capture by Napoleon, The Emperor later installed his sister, Elisa Bonaparte as 'Princess of Lucca'. Today, one of the main gates to access the city is referred to as Napoleon's Gate.

It was three days until the Prague Film Festival, so they wanted to spend their last day this time in Italy very wisely.

They decided they would take the train from Lucca to Florence. The train ride was brief and easy, and they got to see much of the Tuscan countryside.

As they got closer to the city, they began to see red - tiled roofs, more domes of the old churches, then they saw the granddaddy of duomos, the Duomo Santa Croce, atop the Florence Cathedral.

Florence, located in the Tuscany region and known, of course, worldwide for its exquisite cuisine. The girls were hungry and couldn't wait to give the cuisine a try. They settled into a very local type restaurant. The waitress in very broken English suggested something they could not pronounce, but they nodded their heads yes, with a smile.

The waitress brought plates of spaghetti, with a type of marinara sauce, but the twist was a tiny, crunchy, breadcrumb-like topping on it. It looked nothing like spaghetti they had ever seen. As they both dug in, they let out sighs of approval. "I have no idea what this is topped with," said Elizabeth, "but I think I have died and gone to spaghetti heaven."

"This is so good Mom I can't believe it!" It was incredible. Both Elizabeth and Kat agreed it was the best spaghetti they had ever eaten.

While at their table, they took some time to schedule their day of exploration. First and foremost, Kat wanted to visit the Accademia Gallery, where they wanted to see many of Leonardo da Vinci's drafting and drawings on the evolution of man, his first working models, etc. She was glad that Kat was so interested, but who was she kidding? Elizabeth couldn't wait to see it all either.

In addition to da Vinci's works, here is where Michelangelo's original "David" is housed. The girls were absolutely stunned by its beauty and had to pinch themselves to believe they were there standing in front of it.

Then they visited the Uffizi Gallery, where they were struck by so many treasures, works by Botticelli, *'The Birth of Venus'*, Michelangelo, Raphael, and da Vinci's 'The Adoration of the Magi', and 'The Baptism of Christ'.

For their last stop, they shuttled to the Palazzo de Medici, the original palace residence of the Lorenzo de Medici family. With all its architecture set in gold inlay, and original reliefs carved into the walls by many of the famous artists of the period. Elizabeth spoke at the grandeur, "Kat, the de Medici's were the wealthiest Europeans, and some of the first known bankers in history. They loaned money to governments, world leaders and even the church."

Another grand day in Italy. They ate their pizza, hungrily noting that authentic pizza in Italy was nothing like pizza in the U.S. It was thin, with minimal toppings but absolutely, wonderful. Again, climbing the steps to their room, barely, so exhausted from all the excitement. They would be leaving for Prague in the morning.

When they woke, they were both very groggy, finding it hard to get going. This time they ordered their dark coffee drinks through room service. They ordered a breakfast tray consisting of meats, cheese, breads that resembled different types of pizza, and fruit. They slowly drank their coffees and eventually the caffeine took over and they were able to begin functioning again. They had to be efficient as they were booked on a train leaving at 1:00.

When they arrived in Prague after both sneaking in a nap, they were excited to see another city they had been poring over in travel books; Rick Steve's books had become like their Bibles.

Hailing a taxi, and seeing a lot of the city on the way to their hotel, and with their driver pointing out local landmarks, they were awed by the ornate buildings, the history, and the beauty of the city.

Elizabeth noted, "The streets seem so clean. I wish we could find this in America."

Even the air smelled of perfumed lilacs. Many of the people now spoke English, so communication wouldn't be too much of an issue and they had memorized a few key words, in an effort to ingratiate themselves.

Their hotel was housed in an old grey cement building but it was a charming boutique-type hotel, with light and warmth radiating to the street outside as the sun was going down, very inviting.

Two young Czech women checked them in, both blonde, one taller than the other. The taller and prettier of the two spoke near perfect English. They both were very sweet and excited to ask questions about America.

"Have you ever met Brad Pitt? He's so cute." "Do Americans really pay $600 for shoes?"

After chatting with them for a bit, Elizabeth and Kat adjourned to their room. Stepping into the small and slightly rickety elevator, they closed the metal screen and pushed the button for two floors up.

They were greeted in the room by their large backpacks already there waiting for them. They began to settle in; it would be two days before the film festival was to begin.

They took their time exploring the city, sampling the food, falling in love with a local specialty called Knedliky, a spongy, steamed bread dumpling. They experienced the people, who were kind and generous. They toured the Pilsner Urquell Brewery where they were told the first ever pilsner beer was brewed, loving the fantastic and unique taste of the beer served warm. They toured the grandeur of St. George's Basilica, built in 920. They marveled at the Astronomical Clock or 'Prague Orloj' in the old town square. The grand old clock was installed in 1410, making it the third-oldest astronomical clock in the world.

Reading the plaque, Kat spoke, "Mom, can you believe that this clock is over 600 years old? It says that, 'ill fate' will befall the city if the clock is neglected."

"Well, I guess it isn't any wonder that after 600 years it still ticks on!" Elizabeth laughed.

"Sometimes I wish I was born in a different time," Kat sighed.

"You are an old soul, Kitty Kat," Elizabeth said smiling.

There were many wine and food markets to rival the best that they had seen in Italy, smelling of delicious fresh baked bread, meats, and cheeses. There were many specialty stores on the cobbled streets in the little town squares, selling the very best in antique musical instruments and furniture.

They loved the feeling of being in a new country, gaping at everything around them, trying to take it all in, snapping pictures and selfies. They visited local museums, shopped, and laughed enjoying their experiences. At dinner, they tried local cuisine, sausages, and heavy gravies, which they found a bit lacking, but it was a new experience to chalk up.

As they talked in the darkness of their room, both recounting the day, and what they had seen, it wasn't long before Elizabeth heard the rhythmic breathing indicating that Kat was asleep.

7
Chapter

"Good morning, sunshine," Elizabeth called to Kat as she peeked her head out of her covers. This was the day of the film festival and Elizabeth was excited. Today was the day she would see him. She thought the day would never come. After watching so many of his movies, studying every inch of his body in his love scenes, discovering his intellect in interviews, she was finally going to see him in person today.

Elizabeth began to think about what she would wear. She decided she would dress in black leather pants, high boots, and a pink fuzzy sweater. "I want to look sexy and like I am ready to have fun," she said to Kat as she started moving her shoulders in a slight dance move.

"Oh God, Mom, don't dance."

Elizabeth had never felt more confident than at this stage of her life. She had borne and raised two children, established herself in the local political community, she had a lasting marriage, and as it seemed, women of her age begin getting less vain about looks and their bodies. Rather they ease into a calm acceptance of what is and being grateful for the good things in life.

Although this event was taking place in an old, elegant theater, the night was about screening movies, so she was dressed somewhat casually, but added a Michael Kors scarf that set the right tone. She applied her makeup as best she

could, and had begun using some of the application techinques
and brands her daughter had been recommending to her.
Kat was beautiful and looked stunning in her makeup, so she
trusted her advice.

"What do you think, black or black -brown eye liner,
and pencil or liquid?" Elizabeth would ask her. For hair, the
current rage was hair extensions, but Elizabeth's hair had been
growing, and was a good length to just put long curls in it with
a curling iron. This, of course, her daughter immediately
volunteered to do for her.

"I want you to look great for tonight," knowing how
excited her mom was about it. When Kat was a little girl she
was always begging her mother to let her do her hair and put
makeup on her, which they both enjoyed, even if Elizabeth
usually ended up looking a bit wicked.

The first night at the festival was an opening 'gala' for
which Ballantyne would be kicking off the festival and
receiving a Lifetime Achievement Award.

The theater, replete with mezzanine and balcony, with
beautiful box seats, red velvet curtains and gilded architecture
was absolutely, beautiful, Elizabeth thought it was one of the
most beautiful theatres she had ever seen.

It was nearly full when they stepped in after a brief taxi
ride from their hotel. Elizabeth wondered if all these fans were
here for him. Did all these people feel the same as she did?
Although there were many other actors, directors, and movies
being screened during this festival, Elizabeth had already
decided that no one appreciated him more than she did.

She and Kat sat three rows back on the aisle, great, up -
close seats for the event. She whispered to Kat, "Let me sit on
the aisle so I can cross my legs without kicking anyone's seat
with these high heeled boots."

"Mom, this is exciting. I am having so much fun," said
Kat beaming.

Elizabeth smiled and patted Kat's leg. "I just love being
here with you."

The noise volume began to level off when the house lights came down. Elizabeth had a warm glow of excitement and adrenaline running throughout her body, not believing she was here. She was finally going to see him in person and possibly face to face.

When Ballantyne was introduced and came out to receive his award, he was wearing a charcoal grey suit and a lighter grey shirt with a Nehru type collar. Classy but not ordinary, just his style. He took a little bow, smiling.

Elizabeth couldn't breathe. Oh my God, there he was - and looking so sexy, thin and with his side-swept salt and pepper hair. He gave a little speech about the festival and the importance of supporting independent films.

In his proper English, "I would like to thank you all for your attendance, and I hope that you enjoy screening this movie as much as I did making it."

It was an older movie, one she had seen, of course, but loved. Suddenly she had the realization that her plan was so far coming together. He even glanced in her direction from the stage. This was also noticed by her daughter who said, 'Oh my God, Mom, did he just look at you?"

Lying in bed that night Elizabeth begin to think about him. We are both in this small town in Prague tonight, I wonder what he is doing right now. The next day they would be attending the screening of his new movie.

While waiting for the movie to start in a second theater, a little older than the first, a bit less fancy, with cement floors and antique popcorn machines, Elizabeth felt anticipation building. He would be on stage in front of her again soon. She had her sealed envelope in hand ready to pounce if the moment arose that she could speak with him. Watching as the crowd was growing bigger and much louder, they still had about ten minutes to go.

Having a hunch, she told Kat, "Stay right there," that she would be back in a minute.

"Mom," Kat whispered, "where are you going? "

Elizabeth waved her off. She passed through the heavy curtains of the old theater, purple this time she noted. She was surprised to find so many old theaters in this little square in Prague, each just as lovely as the first.

She decided to walk down the long sloping hallway that curved to the right and led to back stage. It paid off!

There he sat on his haunches, smoking a cigarette and waiting for his curtain call. It felt a bit weird to Elizabeth, almost like pulling the curtain from Oz, something you were not supposed to see. He looked small. There he was, just a regular guy smoking his cigarette and waiting patiently.

He almost looked like a small boy with his page boy hat pulled low and suede jacket collar up. Dressed just as she had grown accustomed to seeing him in so many photos and videos; dark jeans, rugged boots, a vest and his ascot, which he always seemed to wear because he loved riding motorcycles, and usually arrived at events fresh off his bike.

But there were many handlers around talking to him and waiting with him to go on stage.

Elizabeth leaned against the wall trying to look inconspicuous. Then the moment came. He proceeded to come up the aisle closer to the stage, leaving his handlers in tow but a bit behind. She stepped close to him remembering now his immense height, and his kind eyes as she held out her envelope. He said, smiling, "Is this for me?"

Grabbing his elbow gently, she said it was a 'hand delivered' from Los Angeles. She smiled and asked if he'd take the time when he could to read it.

With a sort of smirk but kind smile showing all his teeth and making her feel noticed by him, he nodded his head and said, "OK, I will," then ducked into the curtain leading to the stage.

The first thought that registered in her mind, did we just have a moment? Oh, my God... we just had a moment! Floating on air back to her daughter, she was shaking, knees were weak and according to Kat she was very pale. She squeezed Kat's hands and said, "I did it. Oh my God, I did it and we had a …moment."

They sat silently, letting it sink in. Elizabeth was afraid to speak, to lose the feeling of the moment. She remained silent for a while and eventually leaned over to her daughter, grabbed her hands again, bouncing in her seat and said into Kat's shoulder, "We had a moment!"

While Elizabeth spoke, Kat was looking over Elizabeth's head and trying to get a better look at something which finally prompted Elizabeth to ask, "what are you looking at?"

Kat replied, "He was just in here looking around, but he left."

After that sank in Elizabeth said, "OH MY GOD…he was looking for me-he didn't see me." It was just a premonition but she knew he was going to reply to the proposal, but because of the high backs of the theater seats he did not see her leaning into her daughter!

After introducing the movie, Elizabeth noticed he didn't stay. She never saw him in the theater during the screening.

When the film was over, the girls stepped outside the theater talking about the movie, and were struck by how cold and windy it had become.

They took a taxi back to their hotel, shivering and anxious to get into their beds to warm up. Not surprisingly, Elizabeth tossed and turned all night, not believing that her plans were happening. She'd seen him twice and talked face to face with him and now he was contemplating her proposal.

Mid-morning the next day while she and Kat were drinking coffee and sharing a pastry at an outside café, she saw him walking across the square, alone and in a hurry. She watched him as he joined a party seated at table at the outdoor café across the way.

Then she saw them. She recognized his wife and his two daughters, one of whom had a baby stroller. Excited to see him again, and taking in the scene, she began to reflect on his family, and the inappropriateness of the feeling she was developing for him. She felt like a heel.

Elizabeth thought his wife looked exactly as she did in photos, including the most annoying thing of all-she always looked at him like she loathed him. Perhaps it was just Elizabeth's bias, but she seemed incredibly bitchy and not happy. Maybe there was a chink in the armor of their successful 'Hollywood' marriage, because come to think of it, he never smiled in their photos together either. She wondered why they were still together if they could hardly stand one another. The 'kids' seemed old enough to not be the reason. Some things we are just not meant to know, she resolved.

Any feelings Elizabeth had for him, she had equally strong ones about his wife. She sensed that she didn't treat him very well, thus removing any guilt she might have had about pining away for a married man.

Yes, the goal was to get him to agree to write his memoirs, allowing her to get closer to him, but deep inside herself she secretly genuinely wanted a relationship with him, friendship to start, then who knew. The rest of the festival was enjoyable but she never sought him out again thinking he would get back to her when he had more time.

After a bit of shopping, Elizabeth and Kat took a taxi back from the square to their hotel, and Elizabeth was happy to get her boots off. She had begun having pain in her foot from a callous that was developing from so much walking the previous days.

The next day she decided that they would take a break from all the activity and so much excitement during the last four days. Her foot was really beginning to hurt.

She and Kat ordered room service throughout the next day and had a grand day lounging in bed, eating and watching movies and then turning in early. The next morning with her foot still hurting Elizabeth shoved her sore foot into her boots so they could walk to get some bagels and cream cheese they had seen in a little shop, and they went to a nearby pharmacy for ointment that she hoped would ease the pain of the now open callous.

"Ahhh…" Elizabeth flopped on the bed when they returned. "My foot is killing me, I really hope this medicine works."

The rest of the day they spent at the hotel with ointment and room service, watching Doc Martin re -runs and snuggling in bed like they used to do before Kat went away for college. This was nice but they felt a bit like they were wasting away their vacation, and anxious for the next exciting experience.

It was later that evening when it came. The response. The response from HIM! Via email. Looking at her inbox with a message from him, Elizabeth felt a twinge of excitement in her stomach. It said the following:

"Dear Elizabeth,

Thank you for your letter and I'm sorry our meeting was brief. I read your proposal with interest but regret it is similar to the many I have turned down. I have no interest in writing a biography and although I thank you for your suggestion of ghosting it for me I regret my instinctive feeling is that life is too short.

Please accept my good wishes for your future and I hope you enjoyed your trip to Prague.

Sincerely,

Peter

OK, she had struck out. She could accept that. His reply was kind and from what she had learned about him, his response was spot on to his personality. No offense taken. As she fell asleep that night, she was feeling a bit let down and very tired.

She awoke the next morning to the throbbing in her foot. It was severe and unbearable. She removed her sock to find her big toe blue and bloody and swollen. Her foot had basically 'exploded' from infection through the night.

She and Kat looked it over well, and talked it over, weighing their options, "Mom, this looks so bad and painful, I think you should go to the doctor."

"It is painful, it advanced so much overnight. Really though, Kat, I don't want to see a doctor here. I don't know what it would be like, I don't even speak the language."

"Well you've got to do something." Kat finally convinced her mom they needed to get home, fast.

The shortest flight to get them home from Prague had a layover for nineteen hours in Moscow, and under different circumstances they would have loved to get out of the airport and take in the sights and sounds of Russia. She thought what a great history lesson it would have been for Kat.

They didn't speak a lot of English at the airport in Moscow, but Elizabeth was given a wheelchair attendant, Sergei, a large, barrel-chested, greying, stern-looking man, who, as it turned out, was a big sweetheart, and was very kind to them. Elizabeth booked them a room at the airport hotel. "3,600 Rubles please," the pleasant young agent said in her best English.

"Oh no, we just came from Prague, I only have Euros and British Pounds. Do you take either of those?" Elizabeth inquired.

"No, sorry Lady, we only take Rubles," Trying to use her polite English.

Elizabeth looked to Sergei, and questioning she shrugged her shoulders.

"Come, I take you to exchange," said the big man to Kat. Elizabeth remained in the hotel lobby.

At the exchange station, the girl behind the glass window ignored them. Finally, Sergei said something to her in Russian. She sneered at Kat. Apparently, she was on break, but doing nothing. She sneered again at the man. In his stern English, with a strong Russian lilt, "She is American, her mother is wheelchair, need Rubles for hotel -now!"

Oh wow, Kat thought. I'm glad I'm on his side! He cut quite an imposing figure.

After the girl roughly passed the Rubles to him, he looked at Kat as they began to walk away. "Attitude," he said, rolling his eyes. Sergei stepped up to the hotel desk and spoke to the agent in Russian. Again, the girl asked Elizabeth for 3,600 Rubles. It sounded like a lot until she did the math, approximately twenty-five American Dollars.

The big Russian wheeled them speedily down the hallways, this way and that way, smiling at Kat as she struggled to keep up. Finally arriving at their pod, they thanked him graciously for his time and efforts on their behalf. Elizabeth gave him a handful of Rubles, not having a clue how much she gave him. As the door to their 'pod' closed, the girls were left in total darkness, Elizabeth hobbling and feeling around for the light switch, and Kat searching as well.

Finally, they decided to open the room door to let hallway light in so they could find the switch. A bit fearful for what she couldn't see, Kat said, "Mom, I think this is the bathroom," as she opened the door, a barely visible night light shone.

Squinting and getting their bearings, they spotted a light switch near the door. It looked like you needed to slide your room key in it to get it to work. In the dark, fumbling for the room key, Kat swiped it, and the light came on. The room was sparse, but they were tired, and with Elizabeth in pain, they settled quickly into their beds. Elizabeth tried to turn on the over bed lamp to no avail and then the room went dark - completely dark. "Kat, my light isn't working, does yours?"

"I can't even see it-I can't see a thing," said Kat with a bit of fear in her voice.

"Can you make it back to the door? Elizabeth asked her.

Kat slid out of her bed, and felt along the wall until she found the light switch near the door again.

She swiped the card again, but no light. "Oh my God, Mom, it isn't working!" They both laughed but were both a bit nervous.

Then Kat had an idea. "Maybe instead of swiping the card, maybe we should leave it in the slot."

Ding Ding Ding! They had a winner ! They laughed again, such seasoned travelers.

Settling into their beds comfortably, turning out the lights at their will, they fell deeply into a long -deserved sleep.

In the morning, a new attendant came with a wheelchair to take them to their gate. He was younger and not talkative. Elizabeth thanked him with "spacibo," for his help.

They finally reached their gate for Aeroflot Russian Airlines. They were allowed to board first because of Elizabeth's injury. The smiling flight attendants gave the g irls slippers, a blanket and pillow, a sleep mask, and stickers for their mask indicating whether they wanted to be woken for meals.

The flight was long, but both were still tired enough to nap for a few hours. When Elizabeth woke, the cabin was dark and very quiet, most of the passengers were asleep. She opened the console on the back of the seat in front of her thinking a movie might help the flight go by faster. As she searched the numerous choices, toward the end of the list -a Peter Ballantyne movie. She couldn't believe her luck. As she settled back to watch, her mind began to drift back to him. She realized that she felt real sorrow in his turning down her memoir offer.

She couldn't take her eyes off him, forget the other characters, and even the storyline, she was simply fascinated by him. This man, this stranger, had imprinted on her and she wasn't quite sure why.

8

Chapter

After twenty-four hours of being shuttled about in wheelchairs, flying, and waiting, they landed safely in Los Angeles.

Met by her husband, he with a genuine look of concern on his face, they hugged. Elizabeth, feeling his concern and the comfort of his arms, it reminded her just how much she loved him, and made her instantly regret the feelings she was having toward another man.

An airport attendant pushed her in a wheelchair to their car and the family then headed directly to a local emergency room. After what seemed like forever and Elizabeth in severe pain now with a terrible odor coming from the toe, she was finally seen by a nurse asking questions, all the while wincing at the ugliness of her toe.

Elizabeth was taken directly to a bed in the Emergency Department, which was quickly followed by a visit from the doctor. After asking all the necessary questions, he took a swab sample of the wetness now coming from her foot, as a result, of sitting in the plane for twelve plus hours.

"Just try to relax. We need to get you on an IV with some antibiotics and we will give you something for the pain while we run some blood and swab tests."

After the additional pain of the nurse trying and missing her vein two or three times in her attempts to insert the IV, Elizabeth felt the immediate relief from the pain medication they put in the IV. It also made her realize just how much pain she had actually been in for the past few days.

The doctor was followed by a visit from a surgeon fifteen minutes later. Quick for an emergency room, Elizabeth thought.

The surgeon was Middle Eastern, tall and handsome, with kind eyes. He was a Board-Certified Foot Surgeon.

Walking in alarmed, he informed Elizabeth that the toe tested positive for necrotizing fasciitis, a flesh -eating bacteria, and the toe (the big one), had to be removed immediately.

Did he just say 'removed'? She shot a look of horror to Garrett. Looking back to the doctor, she asked, "How did the callous turn into this and so quickly?"

He explained, "Once the callous opened it was susceptible to anything that it came in contact with." She had no idea when and what that might be. Knowing her story, the doctor suggested perhaps walking on a hotel room floor.

The surgeon then asked Garrett and Kat to step out of the room for a moment; then he informed Elizabeth, "We have to take it, and right now because your leg and life are in danger. This infection can easily spread to your blood stream and continue right up your leg. Then we are looking at taking much more than your toe."

What the Hell is happening? she thought. This can't be true. In complete disbelief at what she was hearing, panicking and with no time to think, she was scared and seemingly all out of options. She heard herself utter words similar, to those she uttered when she was told she would need an emergency C - Section to deliver Kat. "Because the baby is in jeopardy" the doctors had said.

"Yes, do whatever you have to just save my baby."

Again, she knew there really wasn't a choice at this point. She said to Dr. Hussein, "Yes, whatever needs to be done."

The doctor was very caring and she could tell he was genuinely sorry that this had happened to her.

She was set up and wheeled into surgery before she could even contemplate the consequences of the outcome. Feeling herself falling asleep with an anesthesia mask over her face, it would be two and a half hours before she woke up in recovery, heavily sedated. They wheeled her back to her room and she slept through the night.

In the morning, the first thing she felt was intense pain. Alone, and the reality of the situation setting in, she began to cry. Would she walk again? Normally? Would she have to wear funny shoes? Your big toe is what you use for balance when you walk or stand she thought. Would she limp? Most importantly, did they get all the infection out? Could she still die from this? She felt overwhelmed and anesthesia and jet lag weren't helping matters either.

When she finally saw the surgeon, he tried to alleviate her fears by answering her questions as best he could, but there were many "it remains to be seen" answers that left her feeling anxious. Fighting back tears as he further informed her that she would be going to a residential rehabilitation center, for about two months! There they would "help you get on your feet again." Did he say two MONTHS? What is going to happen to our vacation? What would rehabilitation be like? Is it going to hurt? Elizabeth's head was spinning.

Two months and some setbacks would eventually turn into three months. Three months of machines, dressing changes, agony, pain, encumbrances, and bad nurses. The rehabilitation facility stunk like feces from all the people who used diapers. She had a mentally challenged roommate, Sylvia, who decided to make Elizabeth her new best friend.

The center was filled with the elderly and permanently infirm. Elizabeth was the youngest and thus very popular among the inmates - patients. They wanted her to join them for Bingo, lunch in the dining room, and craft classes.

The recovery started with Elizabeth having a skin graft, where skin was taken from her thigh and used to cover the hole in her foot that taking the toe had left. During the aftermath of that procedure she was in great pain. She had no idea it was going to be so painful. It took a few days before that pain began to subside and the bleeding stopped.

There were weeks of intense therapy, both upper and lower body exercises twice a day, which led from her not walking at all at first, to a wheelchair, and eventually to a walker, and then a cane. She frequently lost her balance while standing. She still had to take pain medication and couldn't wear shoes, but it was a start.

There were many days that felt endless in the center. She missed her family, her pets, and her routines. Sure, her crazy girls visited as did various family members, her Mom came to town which lifted her spirits, but the loneliness set in during the quiet and darkness of the night.

She spent countless hours reflecting on her life. Where she had been, where she was going. Why, before her trip had she grown so restless?

She felt as though she hadn't really left a mark on the world, aside from her children, and it was something she had always wanted to do. Run for office, or writing a book, perhaps. In the secret of her own thoughts, she also admitted as she had considered before, she really was craving romance, the thrill of meeting someone new. The thought of perhaps having sex with someone new and all that comes with that. Discovering one another, completely. She and Garrett had been together so long that although there was love, their relationship no longer excited her.

She had her computer with her and would occasionally look again at the vacation photos she and her daughter had posted, unfulfilled and a bit sad with the incomplete trip. But she still felt a thrill run through her when she saw the pictures and remembered the sounds and smells, the people, the adventure; and some of the photos were of him.

As she looked at them again, she remembered the smile and intense look in his eyes when they met. He was kind, and she wondered if the little 'extra-long' look and sexy smile was something she imagined, or hoped for, or was it as she thought- he was attracted to her and enjoyed meeting her, too, even though it was brief. She had to admit that she was not surprised by his desire to not write his memoirs, as he had been famous a long time, and the fact that he hadn't done one up to that point had made her think he never would. Still, the look - it was haunting her thoughts. He was smart, sexy, and she wanted him more now than ever. She could imagine herself making love to him. She sensed that he would be very fun in bed, and he had her thinking very naughty thoughts.

She was discharged on the 3rd of July, joining her family for a small Independence Day celebration the next day. Having lost weight through the journey, including muscle mass, she vowed as soon as she could manage she would develop a gym routine, as she wanted to tone up. Ultimately, she would make goals of toning and walking and running three miles a day.

Once given the OK to exercise, battling through the soreness in her foot, it took a while to build up to this goal, but she didn't mind. She was no longer cooped up in the rehabilitation center, and she felt herself growing stronger every day.

Yet somewhere in the back of her mind, she knew she was also doing it for him. Anticipating another encounter was a great motivator.

She reflected on her convalescence and surmised, there is nothing like a life-changing injury or three months in the hospital to shake up your thinking, to remind yourself to live the rest of your life to the fullest every day, reaching your goals and fulfilling your own destiny.

9
Chapter

Fulfilling her own destiny. That's what Elizabeth decided she had to do, and she knew one area she wanted to follow through for sure. Win or lose she had to try. She thought it through, reflected again on the way he had looked at her, and began to write a letter to Ballantyne. She decided she had to tell him exactly what she wanted, as she remembered an interview he gave in which he had said, 'I think people should say exactly what they want'. Throwing both caution and decorum to the wind she wrote:

Hello Peter,

I'm Elizabeth Wells. I'm not sure if you remember me. I was the one who 'hand-delivered' an envelope from Los Angeles, and gave it to you at the Prague Film Festival. It was a proposal to ghost write your biography. I did get your follow-up email regarding your take on doing an autobiography, and I can totally appreciate where you are coming from. It's much more fun to have lived it than to rehash it!

The reason I am writing to you now is closer to the truth about our original meeting. While it is the truth I would still like to write your story, I've put that to rest-but I must admit I did have an ulterior motive in approaching you. However, with the obvious rush in your schedule, and the many handlers, and the presence of your wife and daughters , I backed down a bit. But I am going to be frank with you now. Peter, I am attracted to you in many ways. I find you to be one of the most interesting and intelligent people around. Your thinking fascinates me - it is very deep and it causes me much introspection. Your grasp of history and the world around you, and your knowledge of life's realities and frailties makes me want to know you. My interest is truly not about your acting or your celebrity so much. I feel if you were the guy that owns the local bookstore I would find you still just as fascinating, intelligent, and attractive. My goal is to spend time with you enjoying a glass of wine or a cup of tea, just talking with you, picking your brain, getting to know you. It is my assumption that you have some periods of downtime, as do I, and that we could meet. Of course, I would accommodate your schedule.

Then she took the big bite, knowing this might be her last chance at getting to him.

<u>And then, Peter, I plan to seduce you.</u> As life goes on, I would hate to think I missed an opportunity to share my feelings with you only because we travel in different circles, and whose paths may not have crossed without this effort. I want to get you in bed, but I am not looking for a hot and heavy romp, although that's fun, too. I want to take it slow and easy. I am aware that you are getting older, [my husband is seventy -one, and I am in my forties]. Let me take control of you. I know you belong to the world and you have a public persona, and fame, money, etcetera. But it's the seemingly gentle, kindhearted, animal lover, gardener, that Peter that I genuinely want to get to know.

Then she truly stepped up her game.

I will start by drawing you a warm bath. As you relax, I will light candles and pour glasses of cold champagne. I will soap up a soft sponge and begin rubbing your neck, your chest, one arm then the other, as I gently plant little kisses on your chest, your neck. I will slip my hand into the water and gently massage you and run the sponge over your legs , thighs. I will hand you a towel and ask you to join me on the bed. I'll tell you to lie face down on the bed where I will meet you by straddling you and

*massaging warm oil onto your back, your shoulders, massaging your
head and neck. I'll slide down and run my hands and lips over your
butt, as I massage in the sensuous oil. I'll explore all of you with my
tongue, taking you close to Heaven. I will then ask you to turn over. As
your towel opens I see your erect penis. As I rub your thighs I'll take the
length of you into my mouth. Massaging you and licking every inch of
you, gently gliding my teeth over the head for friction. As you near
climax, I will- stop! Climb your sinewy body, and take you wholly into
me, while you rub and squeeze my ample breasts, and I bring you to a
sweet and gentle come.*

Wow, she couldn't believe what she was writing.
Where had all this passion come from? She felt slightly
embarrassed, dizzy even, but it felt right. He turned her on that
much.

The letter went on,

*Now if this sounds like something that piques your interest, you
decide on what level, as friends or much more, the ball is in your court, so
to speak. I just ask that you give this some serious thought, even if it's just
to sit and chat for a while. I was happy to have the chance to meet you in
Prague, but you were working, and very busy. I left feeling a bit let down,
but hopeful for another meeting, but this time, not about a book.*

Knowing he spoke French, it went on,

*Peter, I have written this in French to hopefully stave off prying
eyes in your world that may see this before you. I have emailed your
secretary and asked her to expect this letter, and that it's marked personal
and confidential, and if she would see that you get it directly.*

Elizabeth

She included her phone number and her email address.
She signed off by saying she was looking forward to hearing
from him. She added a Post scriptum.

Peter, I have never written personally to any other celebrity, and I am writing you based on a hunch, a 'feeling'. I feel the need to be close to you physically, to converse with you, at least once more, no matter how brief. I have not and will not repeat this effort with another. Hopefully this is being kept confidential for obvious reasons as we both also have reasons that mandate the upmost discretion.

She waited two anxious weeks, with no response. Yes, no- maybe…the suspense was killing her. "Here goes nothing- or everything"…she said out loud as she dialed his secretary's office to inquire if he had taken possession of the letter yet, fearful it might have been intercepted. The Secretary confirmed he had not as he had been on film location shooting, but she did put it on his desk and he would be returning to the office in a week's time.

OK, Elizabeth was relieved. She had not heard from him because he didn't pick up his mail yet. She could wait. So many thoughts crossed her mind, how embarrassed she would be if someone else read the letter, or he call and said something mean, or totally ignored her.

Had trying now to live her life to the fullest and trying to fulfill her own destiny made her a stalker? No, she thought, stalkers were unstable and wanted to do harm mostly. She knew exactly what she was doing and what she wanted was positive, and if he didn't agree she'd be OK with that, so long as she got an indication either way. But she knew that facing your own mortality tends to put a hurry up in your get along.

While no contact had been made, she spent weeks trying to decide whether to pursue it. Rationalizing it, she eventually convinced herself that she needed to continue , in order, to get these feelings about him out before she burst. She then began devising her follow up. She had learned about his life and things he enjoyed doing or participating in, sailing, horses, cigars, and would use this information to her advantage.

She sat down one day, and put pen to paper and came up with a poem, an exceptionally good poem she thought. She surprised herself. It was about him, and named thus. It was not about her in any way, simply about his life, his likes, and reflections thereof. Once the wording was just right she then went to the local Michael's Craft Store, with poem in hand, proceeded to pick out a rugged manly frame, an aged, black frame with a thin rope for a hanger, picking out just the right fancy papers and cardboard backing.

Sitting at the framing desk, she spread out the materials and assembled an asymmetrical setting for the poem to sit inside the frame.

She thought it had turned out spectacular, worthy of being hung in a movie star's home or office. She was excited to give it to him, and hoped that it would convey to him her serious interest in him.

The next step was covertly getting the thing in the mail. Hiding her actions and mailings from her husband produced a twinge of guilt - and excitement. Again, she marked it personally and confidentially to Ballantyne. It included a little hand-written card,

Bonjour Beau, {Hello, Handsome),

I'm planning on wearing you down Peter :)-(*With your permission, of course!*) I don't want to scare him, she thought, trying to keep it light. *Yes, it's your favorite mail delivery girl, Elizabeth. These words came to mind when I was thinking about you recently. Enjoy!*

Because I care.

She hoped he would find the poem touching, but not too personal. At this point she was really, just trying for continuity so he would remember and recognize the name and who she was.

She then anticipated her next move in the 'game' she was playing, and indeed it was a game to her with unknown consequences, but that's what made it exciting. She found an online photo of him sailing, sun shining, full masts, beautiful condition of his boat. Searching online she found a company that can put a picture on just about any product under the sun.

She had them put the picture on a decorator pillow, made of fine linen, framed with stunning stripes. Under the picture, she had printed the name of his boat, a naughty but apropos name, "Ready, Willing, and Able". The personalized note that she put with it read,

Hi Peter...

I have secrets, and you strike me as a man who likes secrets. I want to share mine with you. It went on, you know it would be a lot easier to flirt with you by email or speaking with you by phone. I use the U.S. mail so much they want to hire me! Again, going for light. A gift for you- with a not-so subtle message. Enjoy!

Elizabeth

>   *Because I want you.*

Flirtatious, and clearly conferring her intentions, and again familiar, but she did begin to feel that she might be getting too deep, knowing so much about him. Would that begin to creep him out or make him see her as just another fan? Obviously, he had reasons to be careful and reticent.

No, she thought, as she sat at the dining table, noticing the nicks and scratches on it caused over the years by doing crafts and homework projects with her children, which now seemed a lifetime ago, I think I am gaining on him. I have to win him over at least for a conversation. I think this is fun, does he? Or am I annoying him? Without knowing the answer to this question, she continued. Slipping out of the house, covertly smuggling these hidden gifts out of the house so she could mail them, she would feel a quick twinge of guilt, and then a buzz when she remembered who it was going to.

10
Chapter

Elizabeth, now in a mode of thinking about him often, hoping for a reply, checking his website now and again for new news and upcoming films. In her 'real' life the empty nest syndrome waxed and waned. She started to fill her days with trips to the gym, painting classes, and keeping up lunches with her political women's group, also contemplating on trying fencing and other things she had always wanted to do.

Thanksgiving was coming. That would mean seeing the kids for the holidays. She always adored the holidays, the family and friends and good cheer, the warmth of the season, the music, the food!

She would be cooking for Thanksgiving this year, with the kids and other relatives coming over. It was always so much work, but it was always a labor of love.

Overjoyed to see Julian, looking more grown up than last time she had seen him only a few months before. Lots of hugs and kisses, embarrassing him.

"Mom, I'd like you to meet my girlfriend," being so gentlemanly and grown up, Elizabeth noted. "This is Reagan Donovan."

"Lovely to meet you, Reagan," Elizabeth said shaking the hand of the light skinned, beautiful red-headed young woman. "Welcome, welcome. I'm so glad you guys made time for us," lightly slapping Julian's cheek, in an effort, to admonish him for never coming home.

"Well Mom, Reagan is very special to me and I wanted you to meet her."

Elizabeth thought, Oh, this must be serious. "So, tell me, Reagan, what are you studying?"

"I'm majoring in Biological Science with an emphasis on Neurobiology. I'd like to be a Forensic Psychologist."

"Wonderful, good for you." Bright and very pretty, winning combination, Elizabeth thought. "So, that means you will go on to get a Master's Degree?" Elizabeth pressed.

"Actually, I plan to go on to get my Ph.D. as well, but I am not sure I can keep going with school that long without getting tired of it," Reagan said laughing.

"One semester at a time, you'll get there, sweetie. Do you know how to cook? I'd love to enlist your help in the kitchen for the feast."

Julian in protest, "Mom, we are on vacation."

"No Julian, I love this stuff," said Reagan, rubbing his shoulder.

"I like her already," Elizabeth said with a smile. "Dad's in the family room, Jules, watching a game. Why don't you go join him? Here…," handing him a yellow ceramic bowl of Garrett's favorite kettle-cooked chips, "take these with you. He's already complaining he's hungry."

Julian leaned over, kissed Reagan on the lips, turned on his heel, kissing Elizabeth on the cheek as he left.

"He's really a good boy," she said in a whisper to Reagan, smiling. "Have you met Kat yet?"

"Yes, actually we got together with her and John -I don't know his last name, he's Daniel's brother? For dinner and a movie one night in New York City."

"Was it a date, date? I didn't even know she knew John. See we parents are always the last to know," Elizabeth said with a wink.

"So, Mrs. Wells, Julian tells me you are heavily involved in politics?"

Elizabeth finished slicing celery for the stuffing and wiping her hand on a towel. "Oh, I dabble. I enjoy it. It makes me feel a part of the process."

Reagan was snapping green beans into smaller pieces. "My dad is a City Councilman in my hometown -Aspen, Colorado."

"Ahh, wonderful. I'd love to meet him sometime."

Finally wrapping up the cooking, Elizabeth settled down to the Thanksgiving table, ready for her wine. After everyone started digging in, Elizabeth asked casually, "So Kat, how's John?"

"John? John who?" Kat asked with a bit of a smirk.

"Daniel's brother," Elizabeth said, also with a slight smirk.

"Oh, My God-how did you know about that?" Kat replied with a bit of a blush in her cheeks.

"A little birdie told me," said Elizabeth smiling. Kat immediately shot at look at Julian.

"What? It wasn't me!" Julian looked insulted.

Garrett, clearing his throat, said "Is this someone I need to be worried about? Tell him to come see me, we'll go duck hunting."

"Dad! Really you guys, it's nothing, a couple of dates, that's all. Besides I am also dating a girl."

"A girl?" Elizabeth said nearly choking on her wine and trying hard not to show surprise.

"Yeah, she's awesome," Kat replied. "Her name is Marni and she's studying Econ."

Steadying her voice Elizabeth went on, "I -had no idea your interest lay there."

Kat adopted a broad smile and said, "Where, Econ?"

Garrett spoke again, "Does she hunt?" setting the whole family to laughter and lightening the moment.

Kat's poignant reply, looking directly at Elizabeth, "Well, we all have our secrets, don't we?" with a sly smile.

Elizabeth, turning to the reason for the day, "I want to give thanks today for having my babies and loved ones around me, our health, new friends," looking at Reagan, "my children's happiness, my remarkable husband, and all the good things life has to offer." Raising her wine glass, "Cheers."

"Here, here," and clinking glasses around the table.

This tended to be a busy time of year for Elizabeth, but on chilly nights, after her husband retired for the evening, she still loved to download movies and watch them into the wee hours. She wasn't stuck on 'his' movies anymore, she would watch whatever she came across that sounded like a good one.

She hadn't gotten a response from Ballantyne. She had days where she really felt that he would call one day, other days she was not so sure.

One thing was for certain, she was not going to give up until she got a response. Life was too short to just let it lie there. The way he looked at her when they met in Prague whispered to her to keep going.

Thus, plan "C" began to take shape. Her thought was that men who are trying to woo a woman ply her with gifts, and although she had sent two gifts over a period of time Christmas was coming - she knew he liked Christmas, too. He was booked to sing in and around Europe, in Christmas pageants or church services, etc.

As she painted her toe nails in the window -seat of her bedroom, she was daydreaming about him, his smile, his body, which she had seen all of in one of his movies, and thus 'Operation Twelve Days of Christmas' got underway.

She was excited. She would give a gift for each of the twelve days, all wrapped in a tower of gifts she thought he could appreciate. Thinking about him opening the gifts, gifts she had selected just for him made her happy, she wished she could be there to see him open them.

Covertly buying, ordering, and hiding the presents became a matter of hide and seek, but because it was

Christmastime, everyone expected that she would be trying to hide gifts from the kids and her husband. As long as they didn't find what else she was hiding. Sitting at her computer with her new homemade recipe of vanilla iced coffee, with each gift she searched for she felt a fear of discovery, but it also got her blood flowing with excitement.

For the 1st day of Christmas, she had found a picture of him online, playing a guitar, his slim, sexy fingers, the concentration on his face, his greying hair, and bracelet. A nice look, she thought; she had this photo put on canvas. It turned out exceptionally beautiful and she thought for sure this would elicit a response from him. The note she slipped in with it read:

Salut, Bebe.

There is just something about those hands - the thought of them touching me makes me shiver!

She was now in full seduction mode, regardless of the consequences, throwing caution completely to the wind.

Her 2 nd day of Christmas gift was a lovely, famous maker woolen and cashmere scarf, something she knew he wore often. It was luxurious to the touch, and had hints of blues and greens. She wrote:

I think you will look fantastic in this. Let me know what you think.

The 3rd day, a gold, engraved Zippo lighter with his initials and a variety box of his favorite brand of cigars. The note read:

Because I don't know what your flavor is-yet.

Day 4 brought an embossed leather sign, with a saying about his favorite motorcycle brand. She noted:

I am ready for a ride whenever you are.

A clear double entendre.

The 5th day of Christmas, no 'five golden rings' here, rather she gave him a book of poetry by a poet she had heard him mention before.

As she thumbed through the book she imagined him fingering the same pages and reading the same words. It made her feel closer to him in a way.

For the 6th day she gave him casual bracelets, as he had been known to wear. She wrote:

Because they make you look mm...mmm masculine.

For the 7th day, she hoped he wasn't going to get tired of opening them, was an old Playbill of a play he had been in many years before. She looked closely at the pictures of him in it, wondering what he would have been like as a young man. She could almost sense his passion for acting and the hunger of a young man for success. She said to this:

A stroll down memory lane for you, and you look absolutely , adorable in the cast photo.

On the 8th day she gave him another picture of himself, this time with his horse. The attached note read:

A fine-looking specimen-the horse isn't bad, either.

The 9th day she gave him a handmade Tibetan necklace, and asked him to"

Wear it in a public photo.

On the 10th day she gave him a mother of pearl harmonica, an instrument she had read he played for many years, hoping that if the stars aligned, she one day might actually get to hear him play it.

The 11th day brought him a leather-bound journal with his name embossed on it. The note read:

For thoughts and ideas or letters-to me.

The 12th day and the 'piece de resistance', were lovely black silk boxer shorts. The card left no room for guessing:

For a <u>very</u> happy new year. I want to see you in them-and nothing else.

Because I want you to want me.

11
Chapter

Finding herself daydreaming about him, she mused, he was a handsome man, but when he smiled, all the world noticed. For her it was his eyes that had a story to tell. In them she devilishness, the thirst for knowledge and touched her through his words and movies so deeply? Nothing like this had ever happened to her before, but she really couldn't answer the question. She was clearly not looking for a long-term relationship. She was married, he was married, and to her knowledge they both wanted it to stay that way. Rather, she just wanted to spend a few precious moments with someone she found so interesting, and sexy.

She had passed over a few men and had been good to her husband but at this stage of her life she felt that in some way, perhaps with twisted logic, she had earned the right to take something for herself. So, this is what she was taking. She wanted him, and so she was committed to try and make it happen.

After the first of the year, it was announced he would be starring in a theater production in London in the spring. Garrett knew that she and Kat had planned to return abroad after Elizabeth's foot was completely healed. So, she thought selling the trip to Garrett wasn't going to be hard.

Her daughter, on the other hand, asked "Are you sure you are up to it, Mom? You gave me a good scare last time."

Elizabeth answered, "I want us to return because we didn't finish our trip, and I am healthy now and I am still excited about it, aren't you? Oh, and by the way, Peter Ballantyne is in a play in London I would like to see."

"Ah ha-I see," Kat stated. "Are you sure you want me to go?"

"Katherine Anne, that is not funny. Of course , I do."

Elizabeth had already bought tickets to the show. The show wasn't until April, and Elizabeth knew many things could transpire before then, but she was hoping they would be able to attend.

In fact, being from Los Angeles, she knew very well that awards season was upon them and that brought everybody who was anybody to town. So, again she planned ahead.

She sent him another letter, this time with a bottle of Dom Perignon Champagne. The card read:

Awards season in L.A., A drink at Chateau Marmont Bar? Or something more low-key, like sharing this bottle of Dom with me in a private bungalow."

She did begin to worry that men like the chase and she had offered him everything.

This was the third thing he had received from this woman. He vaguely remembered meeting her in Prague, but did remember the proposal about his memoirs. She had sent him a poem, one that touched upon various things in his life. Then came the pillow. She had found a terrific picture of him on his boat, and had it printed on a pillow with the suggestive name of his boat. He didn't know what to think. Was this girl just forward and assertive, or was she unstable? He put her out of his mind.

A few weeks later, when a large box arrived, "Hey boss, this just came for you," his assistant announced, carrying in a large and rather heavy box. This time it was full of Christmas gifts. The note he found when opening the box said that it was for the '12 Days of Christmas', a gift for each day, and that she had fun shopping for him. As he opened each gift one by one each with a little note taped to it, he was impressed. She did seem to know him, and many of the gifts were personal and touching.

As he leaned back in his chair, sipping his coffee, he began thinking, is this girl obsessed, or is she just pouring it on for a real meeting?

He tried hard to remember what she looked like. He remembered the meeting and the proposal, but he couldn't completely remember her face. He did have the feeling that he remembered her to be 'cute'. Not beautiful, but very cute in a playful kind of way.

Now that she had piqued his interest, he began to wonder what he should do about it.

After being away for a movie shoot in Budapest for a few weeks, he was now home for a brief break before flying to California for a few award-shows he would be participating in. He walked to his office, which was in a non -descript building a few miles from his home. After going over phone calls and emails needing return messages with his Personal Assistant, he went into his private office. There on his desk another box from the woman. He recognized her handwriting now even before opening it. He was both anxious and a little afraid to open it. He still didn't know what to think about her, but he had to admit, she did create a little excitement in him.

In the box was a bottle of Dom Perignon Champagne, 2004 a vintage year for which they won numerous awards. The note this time had a specific invitation asking him to meet her in Los Angeles, at the Chateau Marmont. It made him wonder if she was in the 'business', as the Chateau was a famous entertainment industry deal-making spot. She was asking him to her bungalow.

He thought long and hard about what she was asking for, and offering. He always enjoyed meeting women, he was aware of the effect he had on them and their excitement and adoration always gave him more confidence and vigor. Ultimately, he decided he had to go. He had to me et her and find out what she was all about. This woman knew an awful lot about him, yet he knew virtually NOTHING about her.

Yes, he would meet her in L.A., the night of the Oscars. He could handle it, he thought. If she was a whack job he would simply leave.

He went out to the main office, which had various pictures of him on the walls as well as things hanging or sitting about which he had received over the years from fans. There were coffee mugs with his pictures on them, which he felt uncomfortable about every time he saw them, his face, everywhere, but taking care of the office was his assistant's job, and she had decorated it thusly.

"Have we RSVP'd for the Oscars yet?"

She informed him that she was working on it, but had not officially confirmed. He had already agreed to be a presenter, but still had to confirm he was going for his seats. He asked her to confirm and said that he would be going alone.

"Oh yes, I will also be attending the Governors Ball." He thought he would have a quick bite, be seen, then he planned to duck out. "Oh yes, also Becca, make an appointment for me with my agent for the day after. We need to discuss this pile of scripts I have been going over, and book me for the three nights at the Chateau Marmont, a regular suite should be fine. You're a doll. Thank you, love." Smiling his winning smile, he returned to his office.

One of the gifts this woman had sent him was an aged leather journal with rough cut linen pages. He had to admit he loved it, and it now traveled with him. It was embossed on the front with his first initial and his last name, very rugged, totally his style. This woman seemed to 'get' him.

He opened the journal and penned a quick note to her confirming that he would meet her at the Marmont, and would be in touch again after he had his travel arrangements squared away. He placed it in an envelope, sealed it and asked his assistant to get it in the mail that day using the address on her last envelope, a P.O. Box.

12

Chapter

He sat contemplating their meeting. He knew what this girl was after. She hadn't been shy about telling him. His wife had never really been a part of his decisions to stray from the marriage. She had done the same and they pretty much knew that the other did stray occasionally, as long as they didn't bring it home, and they ended up with each other.

He was always a bit afraid of new projects he would be working on. He had a tendency to fall for his leading ladies, so much intensity and working closely together, he feared he might fall in love with someone, and that was not part of the deal with his wife. In his career, he did in fact fall in love with a leading lady, but she was married and had a young son, and although they had slept together, and she had similar feelings for him, she said that it couldn't go on She needed to be with her family. She had long blonde hair, high cheek bones, she was gorgeous, a body like a goddess, and when they made love it was exceptional.

It didn't take much for him to fall in love with her. It did make the filming of their movie a bit awkward as they didn't want the crew getting a whiff of their relationship.

It took a while for him to get over that relationship, but secretly he was happy that he could get out of it without his wife knowing he had truely fallen for another woman.

Nothing like a stiff three fingers of Scotch, and a cigar. Though he had given up his smoking habit recently he still treated himself occasionally to a fine cigar. This was like his bath time, a few moments he took for himself and enjoyed the drink and a smoke. It made him reflect on his father. He had enjoyed both as well. He missed him. His father was a true English gentleman until he started drinking too much. He missed his mother. He knew she had put up with a lot in their marriage.

His mind drifted to his brother and sister. They were both older then he, and getting on and he hadn't seen them in a while. He would have to make some time soon to see them. He really did miss them.

He had enjoyed a long career in theater, film, and even television. He dressed well and it was good for his career, as he still did a lot of fashion modeling. But he was beginning to feel his age now, his body and his face changing and also due in part to the types of roles he was now being offered. The father, grand-father, but he was also getting offered parts as solid, strong leaders.

He had to get his skin reconditioned more frequently now, and was wearing his hair shorter and shorter; his fans expected handsome, he had to give them what they wanted.

He was often told that he was still handsome and he too saw it some days in the mirror. Other days he only saw the folds in his neck, or the age spots on his hands, but he did think his aging was making him a better actor. He felt as though he wasn't nearly as vain as he had been when he was younger. He had settled into his life, not having as much to prove, he was confident in his acting ability, and just tried to enjoy the process now.

His mind drifted to her. He wondered, what is it this girl sees in me? Why does she feel the need to reach out to me? There are many other, younger, more attractive actors out there that a younger woman could easily fall for. He did, however, have a reputation for not being a 'typical' actor. He lived unconventionally, out of the box so to speak, a little devil - may-care and he had a reputation for answering to no one other than himself. This had attracted women to him over the years.

As he began thinking about her, Elizabeth Wells, after re-reading her letters, he felt himself get a bit excited physically by some of her blunt wording, and a little more interested in meeting her. But he worried a bit as he had not had a sexual relationship with another woman in nearly three years, and he was feeling every bit his age. He knew the effect he had on women, but had to be vigilant as to their intentions. Many just wanted access through him. Sometimes he was OK with that if he found her attractive, and he'd let her use him. Other times he felt he could never trust that anyone was interested in him, in knowing him, and not for their own gain. This woman wrote as if she understood that, and claimed to be interested in him. Maybe she was worth the response.

13
Chapter

Opening her P.O. Box, which was an everyday ritual, not out of the ordinary, except this time. There was a letter - from him! She could not believe it, opening and unfolding it in a flurry. Both anxious and afraid of the answer.

'This Dom is a very good vintage and, yes, I'd love to share it with you-in your bungalow.' Her brain screamed, he said yes, he said yes! It went on, *the Bar Marmont always has too many people and prying eyes. I'll contact you once again when I have my travel plans together.*

Best,

Peter

He said yes…he said yes….Oh My God…he said yes! Elizabeth had never been so excited by a letter.

Once the disbelief that he actually agreed to meet her wore off Elizabeth began counting down the days until they would meet-with each passing day feeling more anxious and excited.

On the day of the awards she had been late dining in the restaurant at the Chateau Marmont, enjoying their famous and wonderfully spicy crab cakes, with their award -winning, homemade tartar sauce, rumored to be the best that can be found on the west coast, and sipping a glass of White Zinfandel, which she observed was actually red -well, pink.

She began noticing that the crowd in the bar seemed to be getting louder and growing and the dining room became be-spotted with men in tuxedoes of various shades, but mostly traditional black. They were accompanied by some of the most beautiful women with the most amazing gowns, all by ultra-famous designers, Elizabeth thought.

With this she knew that the time was coming, and she should retire to her bungalow, and wait for the 'moment'.

She collected her credit card from the black leather book that contained her copy of the check. As she slowly pushed in her chair she attempted to nonchalantly scan the room, and yes, there were famous faces at some of the tables and booths, and they were starting to really drink and laugh and have a good time. Meanwhile she had a nervous feeling in the pit of her stomach. Would he show? Does he only wish to meet and talk? Would they have sex?

She exited at the back of the restaurant, taking the brick stairs carefully and following the path created by hedges and flowers. She knew the Chateau Marmont is known especially for the privacy of its bungalows, with a private side street entrance for those who really don't want to be seen. Many a Hollywood scandal had taken place right here, she thought, as a huge wave of guilt crossed her mind. She pushed it away by reminding herself, I deserve this night.

In his follow-up email Peter mentioned something about having to make an appearance at the Governor's Ball before he would arrive at the bungalow.

With each step she took her heart began to beat faster knowing that the time was growing nearer. In a way, she was feeling trapped by a snare of her own making.

She tried to calm herself by searching in her Prada bag, authentic, but a gem found at the Goodwill, for her room key. Was it a coincidence that she got bungalow 8, her favorite and lucky number? She thought about settling down with another glass of wine.

The ivy-covered wall, which had roses entwined that were in beautiful bloom, reds and pinks poking out from the ivy and trellis on either side of the walkway and door. Beautiful, she thought as she remembered just how much this room was costing her. Here she was now spending money on herself that she would normally spend on her family, another pinch of guilt.

She turned the lock and opened the door to bungalow 8. Light and airy with a very spring feeling even though it was mid-February and still a bit cool. The walls were white and bright yellow, the living room was decorated in a sparse but just right kind of way, with a sofa and a side chair. Current magazines lay on a table, noting one with a picture of Ballantyne on the cover.

He had seven movies coming out over two years, not bad for an 'aging' actor. His movies were never blockbusters, and usually played to a more cerebral crowd, but last month, one of his two blockbusters thus far, had beaten box -office expectations with a large cast of who's who.

It put him squarely on the map again for all young and old to see. She felt a twinge of jealousy after that thought.

He was hers, she wanted him. She wanted him in a carnal, lust-filled way. She'd had the 'hots' over the years momentarily for other famous men, but this feeling she had for him engulfed her mind and body. She needed to feel his touch, and no other.

The kitchen was well maintained and airy with a lovely breakfast table, fresh orchids in the vase. She opened the full - sized refrigerator, happy to see it stocked with soft drinks, booze, mixers, and her favorite, wine. Another opening from the kitchen led to a short hallway, then to the bedroom.

The room's centerpiece was a large, beautiful, king - sized bed. Outfitted with thick comforters in white, it had a dozen or so decorator pillows, large with elegantly monogramed "M" stitched in silver, beautiful script writing, all looking so inviting she almost wanted to just fling herself face down in the lusciousness. She decided instead to have that glass of wine she had promised herself, thinking it wouldn't hurt in settling her nerves, too.

She reached in the cupboard to find the finest crystal bar ware Ireland could make. Noting it's heaviness and afraid to break it, she carefully set the glass on the counter. Finding an electric wine opener situated on the counter nearby, she filled her glass.

As she slowly walked around the bungalow again, this time stopping to see the elegant bathroom, it looked like a professional spa, she was impressed, easily noticing a large garden tub for two, surrounded by unlit candles. She sighed. She didn't know how much more waiting she could take.

She felt herself getting buzzed from the wine, and reminded herself to 'slow down, be in control of yourself'. As she opened her suitcase, she searched under her makeup and toiletries, then came to a new teddy she had bought just for the night.

Now regretting the decision because she was planning on opening the door wearing it, she wondered now how would he, or they react if his intentions had nothing to do with intimacy?

After a few moments contemplation and looking at herself in the mirrored closet, holding the outfit up to her, she said "I am taking back my life, no worries, no regrets. If I look like an idiot, so be it. It only hurts for a little while."

As she undressed to change into the teddy, she felt excited and giggly. Am I actually here? How did I get to here, and now?

Oh, My God, she still couldn't believe it. Peter Ballantyne was coming to see -her. The teddy was semi-sheer in lavender, with ribbons and a little bow on the front and a matching panty. When she started looking online for this naughty and sexy lingerie, she felt sneaky, fearing at any moment that her husband might walk in and see what she was doing, but it made her tingle inside at the same time.

As she applied lotion to her legs slowly, feeling the wine, she began to feel very sexy. She maneuvered her breasts to show as much cleavage as possible, forty -somethings with big breasts need a little help now and then.

She slipped into the bathroom with her Victoria's Secret toiletry bag, and dug around to find her favorite perfume, Amazing Grace by Philosophy, slowly dabbing a bit behind each ear and in the hollow of her neck, thinking how oddly old Hollywood that made her feel.

"OK, Elizabeth, make-up good? Check. Breath good? Check, if you like wine. Boobs good? Check. She pulled out her favorite lip gloss, when the knock came at the door.

"Uhhh," -she let out an audible gasp. Oh my God, is this real? Is that man outside my door? The thought took her breath away. Rationalizing, he probably sent his 'people' to tell me he wasn't coming. If I open the door and it's not him, well, I'll just open it a crack so they can't see my skimpy outfit. She slowly and coolly walked to the door, turned the lock and hoped for the best.

She heard the 'pop' outside the door. She quickly opened it to find, her man, with champagne flowing from the bottle over his hand, down the front of his stunning white tuxedo shirt with rich black beaded -buttons, grinning. "Did someone here order a bottle of Dom Perignon from London?"

She thought she would faint. He was sexy. Smoking hot sexy. And that accent.

He stepped into the room, towering over her, he looked her slowly up and down, stepped close to her and with his rich English accent, growled, "Oh, you were waiting for me."

That was it, what she needed to hear. They weren't just going to 'play' friends, he wanted her, too.

He wrapped his long fingers around the side of her neck, shutting the door with his foot. He pulled her close to his chest, champagne still flowing, looking down into her eyes. "You've been working on your little scheme a long time. You don't disappoint."

He warmly and gently kissed her with the softest lips. He said, "You smell amazing", sliding his hand from her neck to her waist, then to her butt, squeezing it, kissing her again, this time passionately tonguing her mouth with greed. He bit her lip gently as he pulled away. When he stopped she heard him sigh into her ear, he was excited, too.

"We'd better find some 'glosses' for this rare and divine champagne." His English accent and deep voice were enough to make her weak in the knees. As he followed her to the kitchen, a quick thought popped into her head. I am going to fuck the great Peter Ballantyne. That heady thought, and the wine she had already drunk made her lean into and grab the counter.

"Are you all right, love?" he drawled in his proper English.

She turned to him, looked him squarely in the eyes. "I'm better than all right. I am here with a man I find fascinating, enthralling-sexy."

Smiling, he handed her a glass of champagne, took his in one hand and reached for her other hand, and without a word, he led her to the bedroom.

"Your letter, which got me very excited by the way, said you were going to take control of me. I don't know whether to be excited or afraid."

He smiled, while turning his head slightly and looking into her eyes. There they were, the eyes she knew had stories to tell, and now he had them set on her. The intense look in his eyes made her think of the guitar picture and the comment about his hands that she had sent him.

"Oh good, you brought them," she said.

"Brought what?" He looked puzzled.

"These hands," lifting his free hand in hers, "these delicious," gently kissing his hand two then three times, "hands."

He took a big mouthful from his glass, then set it on the night table and reached for her glass. She was still admiring his beautiful tuxedo with the bow tie hanging loose, sideways, studying the ring on his hand, one that she noticed he always wore, even in his movies.

Turning back around, he said, "But there is one thing I should tell you, love."

Oh God-was he sick? Feeling every drop of alcohol and the courage that comes with it, she wrapped both arms slowly around his neck, in a sexy, I want you , kind of way. She whispered, "What's that?"

He gently brought her hands around in his, then pushed her down on the bed. In his low growl, "There is still plenty of petrol in this old tank."

As he began to remove his jacket from his shoulders, she saw them-his suspenders. He now could do whatever he wanted with her. This was her weakness, not with all men, but him.

The black leather straps hooked to the inside of his pants, he slowly removed one arm then the other, letting them hang at his side. She rose to her knees to meet him. Slowly she began to unbutton his shirt with her long fingers, nails varnished in a shiny pearl. As she unfastened each button, she planted small gentle kisses on his neck, chest, stomach, while he lightly moaned at the touch.

Sliding her hand down to unbutton his pants she could feel and see that he was ready to take her. He pushed her back down, taking her two hands above her head. He had been working to get his pants off. He was now naked, but for his unbuttoned tuxedo shirt.

God, he was sexy, she thought.

He planted kisses and began licking her breasts as he untied the ribbon holding them in the teddy. Rubbing them he uttered, "Oh God, you're beautiful."

Burying his face in her cleavage, with one hand sliding down to her stomach, down her side and between her legs, he gently slid two fingers into her, looking for the wetness which no doubt he would find. After massaging her with his thumb, he slowly guided himself into her and plunged deeply inside, fully erect.

She let out a breathless sigh, enjoying being filled up with his warmth and the closeness of their faces. For not knowing each other very long in person, they locked eyes easily with passion, smiles, and kisses. He began rocking, faster and faster. She wrapped her legs around his waist, feeling every thrust with pleasure, he, squeezing her large breasts, while enjoying her, with a few of his minor grunts.

"Peter," she whispered as he came. His warmth filling her up. As he lay there with his head on her breasts, she ran her fingers through his hair, the same hair she had seen on the magazine cover on the table.

After a few recovery minutes, he slowly began to slide down her body, with a smoldering crooked smile. "It's your turn now."

He kissed her belly while his hands moved up and down her thighs, kissing and licking slowly while massaging the inside of her thighs, then her lips. He parted them again, starting with small circles then larger, faster, his thumb joining in to massage her clitoris, getting her primed for what came next.

He slid to his knees on the side of the bed. Gently he slid in his warm, soft tongue, licking slowly at first, making her writhe with an overload of pleasure. He stuck his tongue in deeply, then slid it up to find her clit, gently flicking it in a practiced way, then faster, faster until the sounds of pure ecstasy came from her mouth. He returned to her mouth ferociously, kissing her like his possession, then to her neck again, stopping on her 'magic spot' that made her melt and that allowed him to do whatever he wanted with her.

She ran her fingers over his face, over the mole, and the cute smile lines she had gotten accustomed to on all the pictures of him online. For this moment, she owned them. Up close she could see the sure signs of an aging man, folds of skin on his neck, deep crow's feet around his eyes, small, light sun spots. But God had been good to him. He was still a very good - looking man, and she knew many women agreed.

She nudged him to roll over. Now with her on top, she began kissing his face, his ears, his neck, lingering on his neck, she felt like a teenager as she left a tiny spot of broken blood vessels as she enjoyed aggressively kissing his neck and he smoothly ran his hands over her back and ass, squeezing her cheeks.

She moved his hands from her ass and guided them above his head. She parted his lips with her tongue and engaged him in a luxurious, hungry kiss that seemed to last forever. He was a great kisser.

She knew by instinct he was not ready yet for another round. She asked him to turn on his stomach, and she reached for the designer hotel lotion she had found in the bathroom. Rubbing and massaging it into his skin, he moaned with pleasure-he'd had a long day, and he was enjoying this.

After only what seemed like a few minutes, he turned over, fully erect again, it made her wonder if he ever took Viagra. His penis was beautiful, she thought, long to match his tallness. He was uncut, which she had assumed mainly because he was British, that he had a 'turtle neck' when not erect, a term she and her 'crazy girls' used whenever talking about an uncircumcised man.

At that moment, she wanted badly to lick him and make him come in her mouth.

As she lay on his chest, kissing him, rubbing his chest

with her fingernails, she noted his sinewy body had no extra fat and was deliciously toned. He'd always been exceptionally slender, but muscular.

As she slid her hand down, massaging, and gently pulling, he let out a series of moans. She rubbed his thighs, first the outside then the inside, getting him more excited. She slid down and took the length of him into her mouth. Long periods of licking and sucking made him feel as though he had died and gone to Heaven.

She began to move faster up and down the shaft while gloriously licking him and fondling him. He grabbed the tops of her shoulders to steady himself. As he began to moan, "Yes. Oh yes," she felt the warm sticky taste as he came, and decided at that very moment to swallow. She knew that men really liked it, but she rarely did it because she could never really stomach it, but this was fucking Peter Ballantyne. It went down like sweet honey.

He lay splayed and spent on the bed as she crawled up to him, resting her head in the crook of his shoulder. He wrapped his arm around her, and they both settled down into a nice rest.

14
Chapter

When she awoke the next morning, it was to the sound of the Keurig espresso machine in the kitchen. She saw him move swiftly about, already dressed, his suspenders hanging at his side. I wish he'd stop doing that, she thought.

He waited patiently in front of the pot for his espresso to be done, stretching out his sleeves and fastening his cuff links, one then the other. He fixed and drank his small cup of espresso standing up in the kitchen. He's in a hurry, she wondered why? He picked up his jacket from a chair, tossed it casually over his shoulder and grabbed a green apple from the complimentary fruit bowl. Keys in hand he came to her.

"Good morning, darling," in that voice.

"Hello," she whispered with a smile.

He bent to kiss her, softy, sweetly. "I must go, love. I have a meeting with my agent before I catch a flight back home."

Back home. It began to sink in. He had his home, she had hers. They had fulfilled each other's sexual desires, and now it was time to go home. She thought of her husband and felt stung by the feeling of knowing she had been unfaithful to him. Damn, we should have made a hall pass for our celebrity of choice, she thought.

Before rediscovering Peter Ballantyne, her choice would have been Michael Douglas. She had loved him ever since he played Gordon Gecko in the movie Wall Street, his swagger and cool comments, "greed, for the lack of another term, is good," and "the Chinese are eating your lunch". She smiled as she remembered him wearing suspenders in a few scenes of the movie, she began to wonder perhaps she had a fetish, or a type she hadn't recognized before.

"Well," she stammered. "I ...had a marvelous time with you, amazing. Thank you."

"You thanked me well enough last night, love." He smiled and winked as he turned his head slightly to gaze into her eyes. "I've got to go, but I'll be in touch." He kissed her again, soft and lingering. He turned and headed for the door.

Although last night was amazing, he was a good and giving lover, and had the stamina of a much younger man. Why did she all of the sudden feel a bit empty and slightly used? But he didn't just use her, she used him the same, for mutual pleasure. This is what casual sex is, she reminded herself. She had lured him there and seduced him.

She took a deep breath, then smiled and screamed as she threw the blanket over her head kicking her feet. She felt free in some new way. She felt she now had what she had yearned for. And she had fucked a movie star.

For days, she felt as though she was walking on air. She felt herself smiling often. She would see him on magazine covers or talk shows, with a bit of pride and longing. She smiled and remembered he was hers for a night. Sometimes there were pictures of him and his wife, never smiling, always seeming annoyed. Why does he stay, he is so warm and giving? She wondered. There had been plenty of rumors over the years of him seen with this woman, or that women, but it had been tacitly known that theirs was an open marriage, with her doing the same on occasion. Still she feared the wife.

After settling back into regular life, with her memories to keep her company when she was alone, Elizabeth found herself now and again playing back in her mind snippets of their love making, and how good he made her feel. Her routine included getting back to her 'crazy girls' nights. These women all really cared for one another, and they had even thrown her a little welcome back celebration when she returned from the hospital. They got together for several occasions recently, dinner out for one of the girl's birthday, playing Bunco another time, drinking wine and trying to outdo each other, making everyone laugh.

But things always boiled down to two things when they got together: gossip and men.

Why do women talk so much about men? She wondered. The gossip was usually juicy and half the time wrong, but it was fun dishing.

One of her friends spoke up one night, after all of them having too much wine.

"So, you know I've mentioned my boss Dan, whose been sort of hitting on me." He had made it clear over a few months that he wanted her. "And you know I think he's so adorable."

"Yes-and?" Laura prompted.

"Well, I've given it a lot of thought lately, and I, well, I…" she said blushing and putting her hand to partially cover her eyes. "I think I am going to go for it."

That opened the floodgates to everyone's opinion, advice, and questions. Then Mel spoke up about a discussion she and her husband had recently had about possibly getting a divorce.

"What? No, not you guys," Jessica said with sadness.

Mel explained they had not gotten along for some time now, and were not agreeing on things regarding the children and that they had not had sex in a very long time. After the required discussion amongst the girls, it quieted down, more wine was poured and consumed.

Then in an uncustomary, low, mousy voice, Elizabeth said, "I've had an affair."

"What with one of the oldies in the rehab center?" Laura interjected.

A fit of laughter broke out. Elizabeth was not laughing

"No, recently." She couldn't believe she was revealing this to them.

They were all close and usually talked about anything, but she had been reserved during the discussions about affairs. She never confided in them about watching his movies or the buildup she felt welling up inside her. But today she wanted advice. She might tell them about the affair, but never who it was. She was thinking about him more, and talking about him with them made her light up and the nervous feeling in her stomach returned. Of course, the girls had a million and one questions.

Sitting in the window-seat of her bedroom, trying to concentrate on the latest New York Times Bestseller 'must - read' novel, trickles of rain streaming down the window, the first rain of the season, the smell of fresh brewed coffee in the air, Elizabeth's mind began to wander. Would he want to see her again?

She had carefully created a casual laissez faire attitude with their time in the bungalow, but she couldn't stop thinking about him. She feared he might have taken a piece of her heart, a no-win situation.

They were both married; she adored her husband, whom she was finding it hard to look in the eye. She never wanted to hurt him this way, but a month and a half had gone by with her fighting the feeling to contact Peter. She wanted to see him again. No, she needed to see him, to see if she really was a one-night stand, or was the intensity in his eyes when he looked at her something more?

16
Chapter

She still had the tickets she purchased to his next stage production, *Death of a Salesman* in London, for the month after next. He would be appearing for a month.

She waited until he began his month -long appearance at the theater, then she sent him a telegram.

Peter, I will be attending play Thursday, May fourteenth. Matinee. Front and Center. Tea together between performances?

To her pleasant surprise, there was a quick response, an email. She sat with bated breath at the thought of opening it. This would be her last effort for contact. He hadn't reached out to her in a month and a half, and maybe he was done with her. She had played all her cards and was afraid to be let down, even though she knew from the start that it was a long shot, but she worried that she would never have the chance to be his friend, to chat with him, exchange ideas.

She thought, no matter I already have the show tickets, and the vacation details in motion. Kat and I will have a great time together in Europe again, seeing the sights we missed because of the medical emergency.

The Assistant Stage Manager handed him a Telegram, an old- fashioned gesture but still appreciated in the theater world. It was from her, Elizabeth Wells. He hadn't contacted her during his hectic days of filming, but he had to admit he was kind of smitten with her. She was sexy, smart, and funny, and was bold enough to go after him. He liked that. And the sex he thought had been phenomenal.

She drew a deep breath and clicked on the message from Peter Ballantyne. She trembled a bit with excitement and fear as she read,

E, love, sorry for the belated response, was on set in Budapest. Yes, I would love to get together. Can we perhaps make it dinner and drinks after the evening show instead? I'll leave tickets for you at the box office. I am really looking forward to finally having the time to chat!

Best, P.

A year in the making, lots of planning and wishing and expense to her had finally paid off. I don't know what the future will hold, she thought. Perhaps it will only be this one night of friendship, for which I will be forever grateful, perhaps more, if it is the cards.

To her surprise her husband was very wary of her return trip to Europe. He wasn't sure she was completely healed and strong enough for a journey like that.

He knew how important the trip was to the girls, the bonding and their mutual love of European art and history, so he agreed to attend Elizabeth's follow -up doctor's visit so he could get confirmation first hand of her fitness for the trip. Which the doctor gave her.

"Elizabeth, you've healed up nicely, you should do fine on vacation, just make sure you wear shoes with good support, and take care of any problem immediately and promise to return home if you are not feeling well." Dr. Hussein always made her feel as though he genuinely cared about her. He felt confident and saw no reason she couldn't make the trip. So, Garrett, too, had no reason to say no. They were going back to Europe!

She was so excited to go back with Kat and continue discovering and finally, she thought, she will have the chance over dinner and drinks with Ballantyne to talk about the social issues that he supported or had made public comments about, to find out a little of his personal life, and if he was the man she thought him to be.

At the airport, Garrett made Elizabeth promise to come home at the first thought of any health -related issue, to keep in touch, and most of all, take good care of their daughter. They kissed passionately to prove their love remained.

Their daughter with headphones on was oblivious to the scene until her father gave her a bear hug that made her squeal. "I love you, Daddy. Be safe."

They had learned from their last trip to pack much lighter, lugging a heavy backpack from train to train and to hotels was not fun. Now they easily breezed through the airport, to the British Airways terminal.

They would receive another European stamp in their passports. Both were excited for what awaited them this time.

Checking into the Royal Gardens Hotel in London, overlooking Kensington Palace, home to Prince William and Princess Kate, both were exhausted from the ten plus hour trip, and hungry. They flung themselves on the beds, happy to finally be at their desired destination. They changed out of their shoes and into soft and comfy pajamas and socks.

"What shall we order for dinner?" Elizabeth asked, thumbing through the room service menu.

"Fish and chips, of course," Kat said with a smile.

The adorably cute, young room service attendant gave Kat more than her share of attention as he delivered and set up their dinner tray, smiling at Kat often.

"OK, was it just me or was he adorable?" Elizabeth asked Kat.

"Oh, you noticed that too?" Kat smiled.

"We may just be ordering a lot of room service this trip." Elizabeth laughed.

They ate and settled in for the evening of jet lag. With Kat telling her Mom later that she was bored and was going downstairs to check out the hotel. Elizabeth was asleep when she returned.

The show was in two days and Elizabeth had promised her daughter a shopping spree for an outfit for the play. Elizabeth herself was excited to shop for this occasion.

In the morning, after a quick continental breakfast, they took the tube to the Westfield Station and walked the few blocks to the famous Westfield Mall, an upscale, trendy collection of top brands. The theater they would be going to was one of the oldest in London, a real grand old theater, ornate stairways, red velvet seats. Elizabeth thought they ought to dress well, as this was the theater and not a movie screening, and she wanted him to like what he saw.

They spent the better part of the afternoon enjoying the mall and people watching. The mall had high -end quality products you would usually find at an upscale department store in the U.S. There were also many stores they had never heard of, but they stayed with brands they knew and were more familiar with. Kat found a Charlotte Russe, her favorite store, tried on dresses in various shades and length, checking with Elizabeth with each clothing change.

"Mom, does this make my butt look big? Mom, is this a good color for me?"

They had always enjoyed shopping together and trusted each other's judgement. They would often hit the mall as Kat was growing up, just to catch up on what was going on or if Kat needed 'Mom' time because of a problem or her current crisis. Usually by the time they had shopped and lunched they both felt better.

"I hate the way this fits me. What do you think?" Elizabeth, twisting in front of the mirror to survey herself from all sides.

"Yeah, I kinda don't like it either."

Kat's honesty was always refreshing. "I really like this one, but does it make my boobs look too big?"

"Mom, they are your best asset. Let them look big. You look great in it!" Kat enthusiastically.

They both decided on shorter cocktail dresses, not too fancy, Elizabeth's black and her daughter's a young flirty coral number. Of course, they didn't look complete without jewelry, so off to the costume jewelry store. She bought Kat a lovely gold necklace with three porcelain peach-colored roses sitting at the front. It was the perfect match for a young lady.

Elizabeth's dress being black, she wanted sparkly but not too gauche. She decided on a diamoneque necklace and matching earrings. They had both packed their leather heels so breaking in new shoes wouldn't be an issue. Elizabeth liked hers because the heel was a little higher and made her feel elongated and tall, and her prosthetic insert for the right foot helped them fit as good and comfortably as running shoes.

A quick stop at the pharmacy they had seen two blocks down on their way to the mall. They had both decided on their previous trip that the make-up they sold in European pharmacies were some of the top of the line products.

"Mom, can I get a new lipstick, too? I wanna try something a little bolder more-reddish."

After making their purchases, they stopped at a little boutique cafe.

Elizabeth ordered a decaf Americano. She loved the rich dark taste of the espresso in it. She did wonder if ordering this was a slap in the face of the British. Did they hold a grudge? Actually, they had both felt good in England, and that the British liked Americans.

After Kat brought her chai tea to the table where they had chosen to sit, they settled into casual conversation, about life, boys, girls, her daughter's academic successes, as well as her son Julian's. Elizabeth felt both sad and happy sitting across the table from her now nearly grown daughter. Where did the baby go? How quickly life happens, she thought. This made her think of him. She had spent many years raising her children well, but now part of her longed to be with him again. But what of her husband? He knew little, or acted as though he didn't. This made her have periods of guilt, but it also made things easier, him without suspicion.

A shocking new twist presented itself. Her daughter started by saying, "You know, Mom, I love you very much, and I always want you to be happy." Elizabeth swallowed hard. Where was this going?

"I have been watching you over the last few months, the new sparkle in your eye, and the smile that's on your face. I think you are seeing someone. You know I love Daddy to death, but Mom I want you to know that I understand where you are in your life and the nature of yours and Dad's relationship. I love you both, but I think you should continue doing what it is that makes you happy."

Wow, grown up indeed. Elizabeth was stunned by this revelation. Had she been that obvious? Her daughter must be very intuitive and as long as she didn't know who it was, a married man, she let it rest.

"So, you gonna tell me who he is?" Kat said with a crooked smile.

Taking time to compose her answer, Elizabeth said, "No, I'm not. It was one night and it's over now."

"Wow, my Mom having a one-night stand. Kind of risky though, isn't it, Mom?"

"Actually, it's someone... I have known a bit."

"Oohhh, is it anyone I know? Is it one of my friends' dads? Gross!"

Looking at Kat squarely in the eyes, "I thank you for wishing me happiness, as I also wish you and your brother. Life is too short to give up on your dreams and desires. Next subject."

Taking the train back to their hotel, the car was empty. It was still a bit early for the work commuters to be heading home.

16
Chapter

The day of the performance, Elizabeth woke up in a very good mood. They ordered mimosas, and muffins and croissants, fruit and cheese, a real breakfast feast. It was hard for her knowing that a few blocks away from where she sat enjoying her late breakfast he would be appearing in the 2:00 matinee that she had originally purchased tickets for. She really wanted to use those tickets to see him sooner, but she talked herself out of it, not wanting to appear too anxious.

They began to lay out their clothes and makeup, shoes. She felt a fit of butterflies in her stomach and a physical thrill when she thought about seeing him again. "I sent him an email. He is expecting us," she explained to Kat.

"How did you manage that?" Kat was curious.

"He just remembers us from Prague, and the proposal."

"Do you think he would sign a program for me? I want to rub it in my friends' faces. His new movie is about to come out and we are all dying to see it. A couple of them have crushes on him."

Elizabeth, feeling a bit of jealousy to the 'crush' part followed by pride that she had been with him, said, "Well we can always see what happens after the show," knowing a little bit more than she was willing to let on.

"Hello, darling," he smiled, arms outstretched, as he came out the stage door, a gush of hot a ir rushing out behind him. He kissed Elizabeth on both cheeks. "You look lovely. I've missed you," grabbing her hand while she was turning to introduce him to her daughter.

Elizabeth squeezed his hand, he, picking up the hint, quickly dropped her hand.

"Peter, this is my daughter, Katherine Anne."

He reached out and took Kat's hand, gently kissing the top of it. "Hello, love. It's a pleasure to meet you. Please call me Peter."

With a pretty smile, she answered, "My name is Katherine, but everyone calls me Kat. Your show was really great. I loved it. You are such a great actor, I can't believe I'm here meeting you. I have been waiting forever for your next movie to come out."

Peter, smiling, responded, "Aww...well, your Mom and I are friends. I am so delighted she could come to see my play."

Elizabeth spoke, "Peter, you were magnificent. The role of Willy Loman was written for you."

"Thanks, love," he said with a broad smile.

Rubbing his hands together, "So, shall we dine at the Trattoria Rustica? I really love Italian food and they have the best in town."

"Yes, great. I am famished, too. Sound good, sweetie?" Elizabeth looked to Kat.

"Yeah, sure," not believing the invitation.

He hailed a taxi nearby with a whistle and snap of his fingers. As the taxi pulled over he stepped to the back door and opened it. "Ladies, your carriage awaits," in his deep English voice.

Elizabeth felt as if she was in old England, in the time of Dickens. On the brief ride over, they all made small talk about the weather, the tourists, the play, but not before he leaned in close to Elizabeth and asked, "How have you been?"

At a dimly-lit corner table, he ordered wine from the waiter who he seemed to know well. She wondered, does he bring other women here?

After the wine was poured he lifted his glass and they followed. "Here is to our health," and with a smile, looking at Kat said, "and meeting new friends. Cheers."

During dinner Kat asked a million and one questions of him about nearly every movie he had made, in fact, all th e ones that her Mom had watched that had made her want him. Elizabeth had questions, too, but didn't want him to know the depth of her knowledge of him. Apparently , Kat was a fan, too.

Enjoying their meal, Kat asked Ballantyne, "So what is the difference in technique in acting for the stage and acting in movies?"

"Well, the journey into the character is basically the same for me, but it's the presentation that has to change.

For example, if I am doing a stage play I have to project my voice so I am reaching the balcony and the back of the theater without sounding as though I am shouting, so I rehearse projection as well as my lines and actions. Whereas, in movies and television, you can let the camera come to you, the gestures can be slight as the cameras capture everything, and just the eyes can convey a lot. Also, in a film, you are shooting individual scenes which become little squares that the director and editor cut and weave, hopefully well, into the larger screen, becoming one cohesive movie. We often shoot out of sequence in film, so I am always rehearsing the next scene that'll be shot, but in all cases if I am really 'in' the character's head, my body, actions, and my voice take on the life of the character. I really just have to go with it, and most times I get the presentation that I want, sometimes not, or sometimes the director and I see it differently and we keep shooting until it matches his or her vision."

"I used to be a real stickler about getting every scene right, to my liking, but as I have matured I tend to just do my best and hope it matches the director's idea, and if not , I keep going until I can deliver what his vision is. But personally, I love the stage the most. There is more risk and therefore, for me, more excitement, because if you screw up it is directly on you and that can get the adrenaline flowing, which is exciting."

Elizabeth apologized to him for Kat pelting him with questions. "No, love." He reached for Elizabeth's hand. "She is young and enthusiastic. Let her have this," he said with a wink.

A moment later, Kat announced, "I need to visit the ladies room. Mom- will you come with me?"

The emphasis on the word 'Mom' made Elizabeth feel as though she shouldn't say no. "Uh -sure, yes." She smiled at Peter as she rose from her chair. "We'll be but a minute."

"Take your time, ladies."

The minute they reached the parlor area of the large restroom, Kat burst out, "Oh... My... God," she said. "It's him!"

"What's him? What do you mean?" asked Elizabeth, knowing.

"The man you slept with is Peter Ballantyne. Oh My God, now I see it so clearly. Mom you are having an affair with Peter Ballantyne."

Elizabeth shot Kat a hard look. The sound system was blaring out Dean Martin crooning 'Mambo Italiano', but still she worried. "Shhh, keep your voice down," Elizabeth admonished. She was truly afraid to hear what came next, wincing as if that would make any blow less painful.

Then her daughter said, "That is so cool, Mom. He's a ginormous movie star," in a loud whispering voice. "Wow, how did all this happen? Did it start in Prague?" Excited, "I'm right, aren't I?" looking Elizabeth squarely in the eyes.

"You're sleeping with him. Mom, why didn't you tell me?"

Elizabeth didn't want to reveal to her daughter her own little fairy tale, or her private memories and thoughts of him. She had still wanted to keep that for herself.

After dinner and cappuccino, Ballantyne asked, "Would you two like to continue this lovely conversation and join me for a night cap at my hotel? "

Kat asked, "You live in London, I read. Is that true?"

"Yes, yes, it is-among other places."

She pressed, "So why do you stay in a hotel?"

He explained, "Well, when I am in a stage production I stay in a hotel close by. It makes getting to the theater easier, especially with two shows on matinee days, and its close by when I want to retire. So, what say you two on the nightcap? "

Kat was the first to speak. "Um-no, actually, I can't," throwing her mom a sideways glance. "I've promised to meet up with some hostel kids I met in the hotel bar last night, and the cute room service guy," she said wiggling her eyebrows. "They said there was a pub nearby the hotel where we could play darts, a big deal around here, I guess," rolling her eyes.

"Oh yes, darling, we Brits take our darts very seriously, sort of like your American bowling."

"Ah, I see," she said smiling. "So, if you don't mind, Mom, I'm gonna bow out and go hang with them."

Elizabeth furrowed her brows. "Are you sure you know these people well enough?" She worried about her being alone with people she had just met.

"Yes, Mom, we talked for hours at the bar. Some of them go to college in L.A., and I am a big girl. I can take care of myself. I'll be back at the hotel later. Call me if you need anything." She kissed her Mom on the cheek.

Still, Elizabeth worried about a young girl in a new town, but she also knew that her daughter had always had a good head on her shoulders, and would make good decisions, like the one to leave them alone she thought.

After Kat had gone Peter said, "Your daughter is very lovely she looks a lot like you, and very well mannered. I'm impressed by her mother."

"Thank you." Elizabeth smiled and felt a blush come into her cheeks. Here, she thought, was a good chance for conversation. "And how are your children, you have two daughters, is that right?"

"Yes, yes, I do. They are grown-ups now, hardly ever see them. I really miss them. But we do have special family weekends and holidays which they return home for, but now it's with boyfriends and babies and the like."

Stroking his hairless chest, circling his nipples with her fingertip as she lay on his shoulder reveling in the afterglow of good lovemaking. She, marveled at the grandness of his two-story hotel suite.

He skooched a bit away from her so he could look her in the eyes.

"I'm going on a press junket to Paris this week for my new film. We get put up in nice hotels. I have to work but I will also have free time. Join me."

Did he just ask me to go out of town with him? It didn't fully register. No, I must have misheard him. Elizabeth was unsure.

"Well?" He tilted his head waiting for an answer, stroking her face with the back of his hand.

The realization that he was serious struck like a lightning bolt, but she maintained her composure. "Sure, I would like that," she said smiling. Inside her head, she heard screaming, and oh my God, Peter Ballantyne just asked me to spend the weekend with him. I think I have died and gone to Heaven. The next thought was unsettling. What about Garrett? Working hard and holding down the fort, while she was in Europe fucking movie stars. She knew it wasn't right, but she also knew she couldn't say no.

"Aren't you afraid of being seen together?" she asked.

"Oh, we'll be discreet, but if they do they do. The press is always writing some rubbish about me. I've gotten too old to care anymore."

No, no, no, she thought, this isn't good. She was afraid of them being seen together and perhaps photographed. What would she do if Garrett saw them? No, no, she began shaking her head. This isn't going to work.

Sensing her apprehension, Peter said, "Not to worry, love, I have a disguise."

She laughed. "A disguise?" Raising her eyebrows, "Like a spy?"

"Who knows, maybe I am really James Bond and you are my mission, and I choose to accept it." He rolled over on top of her, kissing her neck and lips passionately.

She threw her arms around his neck, and said, "Oh, James." both giggled together.

She had written before that his celebrity didn't matter much to her. It was him she was interested in, she thought, and while that was really the truth, she had to admit she still felt proud and excited to be sleeping with a handsome movie star.

17

Chapter

On the press junket stop in Paris the interviews with various media outlets were being shot at the hotel swimming pool, sparkling and crystal blue. Good weather, the pool over looking the beach, nice location, Elizabeth thought. While he was busy with interviews in the morning, she decided to strike out to explore the city.

That afternoon she returned from shopping, and burning for him, she walked up to the area of the filming; he saw her out of the corner of his eye while he was talking. She waited anxiously for a halt in the action. When they finally cut to comb the interviewer's hair and dab at Peter's face with powder, Elizabeth leaned in to one of the directors and said,

"I have a message for him, very important."

"Oh yes, please," his arm showing her to Peter in a sweeping motion.

She came up beside him. He was sitting in a cream - colored director's chair for the interview.

He looked sexy in a long-sleeved loose-fitting linen shirt, with a worn denim vest for flavor. Then she noticed it. He was wearing the necklace she had given him for Christmas. That made her feel good. She put up her hand to whisper and he leaned in to hear. He smelled of manly soap, nutty, with a hint of musk, perhaps sandalwood. She said softly, "I'm not wearing any panties under this dress."

He leaned back, serious face, "I see. Yes, thank you."

She walked away in a flippant manner and took up her previous spot to watch. He gave her a sly grin just before the cameras began to roll again. She was already feeling sexy after wandering into a lingerie shop.

No, she had to be honest, it was a sex shop.

She had tried on a few pieces and decided on a black teddy, split in the front, with open holes for her breasts. It was an underwire with a corset, so it held her up nicely.

Then she had meandered into the lube and oils section. There she found flavored body gels, to sweeten up anything. She bought two, the chocolate and the raspberry. On her way back to the hotel, she felt as if every French person she passed on the street knew of her dirty little secret, and that made her even more wet for him.

She enjoyed watching him work. He was so intelligent and easy going. This was what she used to watch on her computer at night, his interviews and appearances not so long ago. Feeling free and easy, and sexy, and wanting him now, she remembered seeing bananas hanging in the Tiki bar she passed on the way into the pool area. She walked over to the bar.

"Hi, can I have a Cuervo margarita and I'll have a banana." She walked in her heels carefully on the pool deck, returning to her viewing perch.

She took a long drink of the margarita, enjoying it. She was on vacation, after all.

With her eyes set on him, she began to peel the banana slowly. He slightly glanced over when they were rolling while he was talking, then he looked again at her anticipating her next move. When she had the banana peeled most of the way down, she waited for the look again. She slowly wrapped her lips fully around it and guided it into her mouth, then took a bite. He adjusted in his seat trying to stay focused on the interviewer's questions. He had his hand over his eyebrow, slightly covering his eyes. It was obvious he couldn't take it, concentrating on his interview, while his desire for her grew, but he glanced over at her clearly more interested in what she was doing.

Knowing he was watching her, she turned and intentionally dropped the empty banana peel, put her finger to her lips, bent over exaggerated, so her dress came up around her rump, picked it up and threw it in the silver trash can. As she began to leave the area without looking back he said, "Cut. Cut! Um- I need a break. This has been a long day already. Please forgive me."

He unhooked his microphone and went after her. He caught her just before she got on the elevator. He got on also and was disappointed to see a third person inside. He glanced over at her and prayed this man would get off the elevator. Two floors later he did. Peter went to her. He began kissing her hungrily. She could feel his excitement rising.

When the elevator stopped on their floor, they separated and coolly walked down the hallway.

Reaching the suite, he took the key from her and let her in. The door closed, and narrowing his eyes, he said, "You, naughty, naughty girl."

She smiled and said, "You have no idea."

He slammed her up against the wall with her hands above her head, frantically kissing her mouth, her neck, all the while trying to feel if she was truly naked under her dress. When he discovered she was, this made him even hotter for her. He lifted her up and took her to the kitchen. He sat her on the counter, ripping open the top of her dress, buttons flying and tumbling down to the floor. Quickly unzipping his fly, he forced himself inside her.

She groaned with pleasure. She had been thinking about this all day. Now he was here, inside her, making her feel so good. He knew what he was doing. Before he came he took her down, she, wrapping her legs around his waist, he carried her to the side chair in the living room. He then turned her and leaned her over it while grabbing and massaging her breasts, he took her from behind.

She was as hot as he was. He touched her in the right places, so when she was on the edge he felt it. He plunged deeper, and they orgasmed together. They laughed together over how frantic they had been, and she turned around to kiss him long and sweetly. "Shall I make us some drinks?" she asked.

"That would be smashing, darling. I've been talking all day and I am parched."

Her dress was ripped and showed her breasts. While she made the drinks from a wet bar, he sat admiring them. "I'm sorry about the dress, love. Let's go shopping tomorrow."

"Don't apologize," she said. "It made it that much hotter," she smiled.

"So, when are you going to tell me what happened to your foot?"

She thanked him for not mentioning it until now. She had often wondered what a lover might think or say. She sat on the floor, legs stretched out and crossed in front of where he was sitting on the sofa.

Sipping her drink, she began telling him the ordeal of her foot. Finally, we're talking, really talking she thought .

They went on to talk about the social issues he supported and his many charitable causes and his recently - produced documentary about ozone depletion, and how global warming is killing the planet, it explained what was causing it and how each of us are contributing to it and how we are responsible for stopping it. She was impressed.

Then Elizabeth asked him to explain the prison poetry project that he supported and had done a Public Service Announcement and created a foundation for.

He explained, "Basically, it educates prisoners on writing and styles of poetry and fiction in weekly writing classes as a way of expressing themselves, calming their behavior by letting out their feelings. The program helps them get their work published as a way to help them pay their restitution payments to their victims."

She knew he had been on a speaking tour to raise money for the program, doing talk shows, interviews, and he was very passionate about it . "I'm proud of you. I think that is a very worthwhile program for which to use your celebrity status." Smiling.

They talked about their animals, which made her a little homesick for her Chihuahua Sophie and Tinkerbell, her cat. He spoke of his horses, dogs, goats, and other assorted farm animals. Ironic she thought. He always portrayed a regal upper - class Englishman, and here he lived like a cowboy.

When the topic of their childhoods and upbringings came up, he became a bit melancholy. She noticed the cha nge, the crease in his forehead and the furrowed eyebrows. He explained, "My childhood was OK, but not great. My parents fought often, my Father drank to excess. But he never hit us, or failed to provide for us kids."

She offered how her father left the family with no notice that he was leaving, no money, and the struggle they had as a result. Apparently, she said, he had fallen in love with someone else, and chose to forget he had children. She was fifteen. This brought bit of a tear to her eyes.

He reached for her hand. "I'm so sorry that happened to you, love."

She was surprised to see that he was so genuine. He was a good listener. She felt the time was right for the inquiry. "Tell me about your wife."

"My wife-my wife, yes, well I married her because she became pregnant with my child; I don't know if I would have married her otherwise. She was a small -town girl from Scotland, and very Catholic. We had to have the baby, and I felt it wasn't right for the child's parents to not be married.

Four years later she became pregnant with our second daughter. We just developed into a family and we had some good years, and raising the kids was fun. But with both of us acting we were apart a lot, and that takes a toll after a while."

"She is also very moody, a bit of a bitch, really, and I get tired of that. But I have to admit I am moody, too. Anyway, as the years went by I began feeling trapped. I needed more freedom. I took up car racing, fly fishing, making more public appearances, mostly for charity. She basically did her thing. We've both slept with other people in our marriage, but we grew into a routine, and you just get used to having someone there, with whom you have shared memories, and a history, you know?"

She knew exactly what he meant. He went on, "So with the girls gone, we basically do our own thing, and come together when our schedules allow."

"Why did you not leave?" she wanted to know.

"The kids, and then more time went by, and over the years we have developed a tacit agreement not to leave one another. She's been there for me when I've needed her. She has understood what I needed even when I didn't."

That was intense, and it made Elizabeth remain silent for a few minutes in thought.

Breaking the silence, touching her foot with his, he asked her, "So, why me?"

How could she explain what she had felt for him? She started, "I've never done anything like this before in my life. I don't go around falling for actors or famous people. I did, however, watch videos of many interviews you have done where you spoke out about things you believe in. While some of them put you in the news for being controversial, I saw beyond that and really listened to what you were saying. I began to see how intelligent you are. Your knowledge of the world, history, and the arts, I just really wanted to talk to you. You fascinated me. Then the more I looked at your films I began to fall for you sexually, and I decided I would do what it took to be with you, at least once."

When she finished her story, she took a sip and looked at him. He had an intense deep look on his face, one she hadn't seen before. He said, "I'm afraid of what you might come to mean to me."

She closed her eyes and brought her clasped hands to her chin. After a few seconds went by, she opened her eyes to see those eyes, those beautiful eyes pointed at her. "I know." She closed her eyes again, opened them and said, "I feel the same way."

"I am trying very hard not to fall in love with you, Elizabeth."

18
Chapter

The next day they went out together, he in his hat and glasses disguise. They strolled through Paris, stopping to look at landmarks and odd or funny things, going into a hat shop and trying on everything and making fun of each other, laughing and having a good time. On the sidewalk, an occasional fan would still recognize him. He, being his most gracious self, spoke with them, gave them autographs, wished them well as Elizabeth casually stayed in the background. As they were walking in silence for a bit, Peter said, "I'm sorry I can't hold your hand."

She replied, "I understand. This is us being discreet."

He laughed a little. He nudged her to go into the next store, a jewelry store. They both browsed, and then he made a purchase, a lovely script "M", bracelet in small diamonds. He said it was his daughter Mackenzie's birthday soon, and he wanted to get her something special.

Later, when they were in a café sipping tea and enjoying little tea cakes, Elizabeth feeling very European, Peter pulled a box from his jacket and said, "I saw this and I wanted you to have it." It was a beautiful diamond infinity necklace. He rose to put in on her. It sat nicely around her neck.

"Oh Peter, please, you do not need to buy me gifts, that's not what this is about."

He said, "Why not? You bought me -twelve." He winked at her.

They returned to the hotel suite, exhausted from so much walking. They agreed they both needed a nap. Elizabeth snuggled under the covers. Spooning, they quickly fell asleep.

She awoke before him. She had slept for about two hours, much longer than she had intended. She went to the kitchen for a glass of water. Then she remembered her purchases. So, she strolled over to the fireplace, and lit it with the flick of a switch. She looked in the linen closets for a few cozy blankets.

She laid them and two large sofa pillows on the floor in front of the fireplace. She opened a new bottle of champagne, and poured two glasses. He would be waking soon, she thought.

"What is all this?" He wandered into the living room, blue boxer shorts and his white oxford shirt completely unbuttoned, showing his belly button. They lay quietly watching the fire, giving each other occasional lingering kisses. After a while, Elizabeth stood up and said, "I'll be right back."

"Hurry back, love, I'll miss you," he growled.

She slipped into her new black teddy, positioned her breasts just right, reapplied some lipstick, fluffed her hair, and spritzed a bit of perfume on. She came to him. "Oh love, you're killing me. You look *very* delicious."

She straddled him, and let him gaze at and touch her breasts, the only thing so far exposed.

"You have the most beautiful breasts I have ever seen. They are soft and large and I love them." He bent, kissing them. He was hard as a rock under her. But she wanted to tease him.

She had brought the flavored gels with her, and laid them to the side where he couldn't see them, so he didn't know what was coming. She sat up and slowly removed her teddy, his eyes smoldering, taking her in as she did. All he had on now were boxer shorts already stretched to the limit by his arousal.

She pulled them down and off his legs, erection springing free, all the while looking at him with her sexiest look.

She opened the top of the chocolate gel and squirted it all over his chest, neck, his groin, his legs, and came up to wipe the rest on and around his lips. Sticking her fingers in his mouth and kissing him passionately, then it began. She gave herself a treat and gave him a tongue bath, which he clearly enjoyed. Small licks that ended with kisses, she licked every inch of his body, with him letting out moans of pleasure. For over an hour he was her dessert.

Both completely naked and wrapped around each other, she had him roll on top of her, and he kissed her. She reached down, feeling him still firm and ready for action.

She pushed up the sides of her breasts. Squeezing them together, she gestured and said, "Come up here".

He knew what she meant. He straddled her upper body. Petting him, she guided him between her breasts, using them to squeeze and massage him. He began to thrust, faster and faster while heavy breathing sounds escaped his lips, she , keeping her breasts tight used them to make him come. Hands against the sofa to steady himself as he came, he groaned, "Oh God, I can't believe you. You're amazing."

"Mmmm," she moaned with a smile. "A diamond and pearl necklace all on the same day."

He smiled and rolled over to rest. "How do you keep up with me, do you take Viagra?" she broached.

He volunteered, "Only when I need it, and I haven't needed it with you." Smiling.

After resting and drinking their wine, she laid back and reached around the pillow to get the raspberry gel. She held it up, lightly shaking it from side to side. "My turn."

A smile spreading across his face. "I don't know if I need that, love. Yours is the sweetest pussy I have ever tasted."

Wow, he knew how to say what a girl wanted to hear. He could charm the pantaloons off the Queen herself.

He began out of the gate, licking her and biting her clit. She was aroused, but he continued. He got on his knees and drizzled the gel over her body, slowly working his way with his mouth from her lips, her neck.

A prolonged stop at her breasts, taking the whole nipple into his mouth and softly using his tongue to kiss them, he would bite at her nipples, and that electrified her body. Wanting more, as he continued to her tummy, then her hips, outer thighs, she thought she was just about to lose it, he licked the curve on the back of her knee, then began his journey up inside her thighs.

She had never wanted a man more than she did at that moment. She hadn't even known this intensity was inside her. He parted her with two fingers and gently used his tongue, licking the walls in a circular motion, two longs lick on her clitoris, bringing her to the edge of ecstasy.

When she began raising her hips to meet his tongue he knew she was ready.

He stopped and asked her, "You like to mix things up, right, love?"

She nodded quickly to affirm, not wanting him to stop.

He whispered, "Here we go." He licked her slowly, full length two more times, and reached for the empty champagne bottle. He gently touched her with the bottle to make her aware of his intentions. She let out a low "mmmm", then he began sliding it into her. Surprisingly, she was so ready it felt good and hard, and cold for a nice change. He inserted the entire neck of the bottle in her, she, moaning with intense pleasure.

He had already found her G-spot with his tongue, and she was ready. He started to move the bottle in and out, slowly at first then she whispered 'faster', until she arched her back and twitched and moaned deliciously.

Afterward they lay in front of the fire, he finally said,

"We're going home tomorrow." She nodded in agreement. "Are you going to be OK with that?" he asked.

"I have to be, I agreed to it. You are married, I am married, and I don't want to hurt anyone." She thought a moment. "But I don't know how to go on while longing for someone I can't have."

He, stroking her hair, "We'll make the time, we will see each other, but I will miss touching you and talking to you, laughing and holding you."

19
Chapter

Having only talked via email, he, being tied up with narration projects and charity events, but she was glad they were communicating more regularly. But she had a hard time getting over him after being with him for a couple of days in a row, knowing that seeing him would be rare, yet she was still thinking about him almost daily. The last time they had emailed he had told her he would be going to Italy for early photos for an upcoming movie project he would be starting soon after. She longed to see him, but would never tell him. Her aim was not to put pressure on him, rather to just hope that they would have more time together later.

Over time things began to get more 'serious' between them them, as serious as it could be with them both being married. Their emails and phone calls became more frequent.

But it was a lovely surprise when Elizabeth received a phone call from him. "How are you, darling?"

"Better now that I am talking to you" she said with a smile sin her voice.

"Mmmm" he replied. "Well, I am really missing you. I need to see you. Come meet me in Wales."

Elizabeth was now starting to get used to taking international flights, an alone this time as Kat was back at school, the crazy girls covering for her, still not knowing who she was seeing. As her fallback excuse to Garrett, she would cite political functions that required her to go out of town, which was not completely unusual .

Another ten-hour flight to London, hoping they changed the in-flight movie selection which had been stuck with the same movies for far too long. Excited to see a new Julia Roberts movie she had wanted to see this time.

The same old food, but she couldn't complain. She actually liked the beef tips. This time she treated herself to a glass of wine with dinner, which eventually mellowed her enough that she was able to doze off for a few hours.

She awoke to the Asian baby in the seat with its parents in front of her, crying. Rather than being annoyed as many of the other passengers let the parents know they were, Elizabeth felt sorry for the parents. It can't be easy taking such a long flight with a little one. She thought. Once they fed and changed him again, he was lulled back to sleep. Elizabeth decided to crack open a book that Peter had recommended to her. It was about the history of the Mayan Civilization.

Peter owned and was renowned for his palatial palace of a home. Located in Wales, tucked away, it was his escape. Out of the way, secure, relaxing.

A place where he could play his guitar, read books and movie scripts. Although he and his wife owned several houses, this was his favorite, his home, where his neighbors let him be a 'regular' guy. He had mostly been the one to decorate it, in a masculine style, with many relics and special pieces he had gotten from his travels to various locations around the world on movie shoots. Unpretentious, no pictures of himself or his wife. Tapestries, rugs, knick-knacks. It was homey, but its opulence was clear.

Peter had assured her it was not his wife's favorite place to be. He felt they wouldn't be disturbed by her there.

Flying finally into Gatwick Airport outside of London, Elizabeth transferred to a train that would take her to Wales.

She loved the Welsh countryside, all the little farms and easygoing people.

Upon arriving at the large manor by taxi from the train station, she was impressed. There was a staff member, short and a bit rotund, with red hair and a lovely smile.

"Hello, welcome. Our boy has phoned and he has been kept longer than anticipated. He will be along shortly. My name is Sally, please come in, love." She reached for Elizabeth's coat.

Elizabeth felt very awkward. Did this woman know why she was there? Did this happen a lot? What would she think about her sleeping with a married man?

The lovely women asked if she could fetch her a cup of tea, and proceeded to show Elizabeth to a guest bedroom so she could put her things away.

Before Elizabeth was finished unpacking she heard Peter arrive. Trotting down the large staircase, she saw him. They locked eyes and he held out his arms for her.

"Hello, darling. Oh, how I've missed you."

He picked her up and twirled her a bit- kissing her neck and then her lips. Elizabeth was a bit shell-shocked, as "Sally" was there still talking to him. Elizabeth felt like a heel.

He informed her that they would be having a small dinner party that night with a few of his close friends, including a gay couple, one of which he told Elizabeth was his best friend.

They had studied theater together, he said. He trusted them immensely and wanted them to meet her. One of them was a famous English advertising mogul, and the other a theater director, though she had never heard his name before. The director much more flamboyant than the other, in fact, they struck her as an odd couple, one energetic, outgoing, with the mogul being a calmer, quiet man. But perhaps, that's why they say opposites attract she rationalized.

The Director, Michael, blond and the shorter of the two, loved to gossip about mutual friends, and occasionally dropped a little insider information about Ballantyne, things like the girls he used to chase, or his hard -drinking days.

This concerned Elizabeth. She wondered, would they gossip about them later? But Peter said he trusted them implicitly, and had known them for many years.

James, the mogul, was tall and well built. He was brunette but had begun getting grey around the temples, but he was younger than Michael. She thought he was quite handsome. These two made her think of the book, "The Picture of Dorian Grey". She wasn't sure why exactly. When introduced, they were very warm and genuine. She initially felt no awkwardness in their presence.

They dined in the small but elegant dining room, with candlelight and classical music, and were served by another employee, wearing a dress, a smile, and sensible shoes. She was also very nice, and she spoke with an Irish accent.

After serving the meal she told Elizabeth, patting her hand, "My name is Eileen. Please let me know if you need anything else, dear."

They all talked easily and enjoyed each other's company. She learned that the couple was in the process of adopting a little girl from Cambodia, for which they were very excited, and tending to all the details of turning one of their spare rooms into a nursery. Elizabeth recounted the excitement she too felt when she was pregnant with her children and the fulfillment she got out of decorating their nurseries. Michael was very kind and attentive, even asking to see pictures of Kat and Julian.

After dessert was served, they all adjourned to the library for cigars and brandy. Peter took Elizabeth by the hand and led her to the library, which was adorned with pictures of horses and dogs. Very English she thought.

She sat down, with Peter sitting on the arm of the chair, putting his arm around her.

She did not like the feeling of being the 'mistress' in front of these people or the staff, no matter how warm. It made her feel cheap or dirty. They wouldn't understand how she felt about him. She did enjoy the warmed brandy, it was quite cold in the upper part of Wales this time of year, and she was chilled to the bone, and would take anything she thought would warm her up on the inside.

She got to hear many tales of the theater and its stars, various Hollywood insiders, and even a few anecdotes about the royal family. She found herself enjoying the evening very much.

When getting ready to leave, hugs all around, Michael whispered as he hugged Elizabeth, "I am so happy for you two. He's a good guy, just be careful."

She pulled back to look into Michael's eyes. "What does that mean?"

"Oh, nothing really. He just flies off the handle sometimes, but you'll be fine."

She pushed the comment to the back of her mind, promising to think about it at another time.

James hugged her, telling her he was very glad to finally meet her as Peter had told him all about her.

"Enjoy the rest of your visit to our fine country, Elizabeth, I hope we see you again be fore you leave." He kissed her on both cheeks.

Peter told them all about her-knowing that gave her a thrill.

Later that night after all the guests had gone, he drew a bath in the large garden tub, filling it with a fragrant bubble bath. He then lit candles around the tub, and brought in the champagne chilling in the stand. He placed two glasses on the side of the bath.

After she finished putting away items from her luggage in the spare bedroom the first woman had shown her to, Elizabeth moseyed into his room. He came up to her, placing his hands on her shoulders. Sliding them down her arms, he pulled her close and kissed her.

"You were wonderful tonight, and beautiful."

"Mmm…" she nuzzled his neck. "Flattery will get you everywhere."

He bit her earlobe. "I'm counting on it. Join me for a soak." He gestured with his head toward the bathroom. Seeing the candle light bouncing off the walls, she knew she was in for an adventure. As she walked into the bathroom peeking around to see the tub filled with bubbles, he put his hand on her back and turned her around, unlacing a peasant shirt she had changed into. He kissed her neck, and taking the shirt off over her head, he began kissing her breasts. She ran her hands thru his longer than usual soft grey and black hair.

She unbuttoned his pants. He stood straight up, giving her an easier access. Then she moved to his tie hanging loosely around his neck, lifting it over his head, then she slowly began unbuttoning his shirt. They gazed into each other's eyes in silence with his head tilting to the side and a smile on his face.

He held her hand as she stepped into the bath, then followed her in. She was so happy to find it steamy warm. She covered herself in the wonderful smelling soft bubbles. He brought up his hand and put a dot of soap on her nose.

Smiling, she asked, "Why are the British so fond of baths? I couldn't drag my husband into a bath, yet the British seem to do it every day."

"Well I don't know about others, but I take one because it's the time of day when I have few moments to myself to catch my breath and relax. You know my days are filled with filming, or junkets, fans wanting autographs, or meetings, and returning phone calls, answering fan mail."

"Uh-oh," she said, feigning fear. "Answering fan mail? Do I need to be worried about that?"

"No," he laughed, tossing a sponge at her. "No one has ever been as bold as you in writing to me."

She said, "You know, you never did tell me what your favorite gift was."

Peter looked up, thoughtfully, "Wow, that's a tough one. You sent some really special things."

She smiled. "Well, I had to get your attention."

"And that you did," he said with a smile. His cell phone began ringing in the chair near the bath. "Sorry, love, let me get this." Leaning back with his head against a large sponge, he answered.

"Hello Darling, how are you my beautiful daughter? Yes, I know, love, I have been quite busy as of late. Yes, I'm in Wales. Sure, sure, yes of course, what time did you have in mind?" He shot a look and smirk at Elizabeth. "Let's make it a bit later. How about tea, 'round three? OK, love, looking forward to it. Bye."

She loved seeing him so sensitive and genuine. She had always known he was a good man, kind, loving, caring about others. "My youngest is missing me. She will join me here for tea tomorrow. Now in the morning, I have to introduce you to Annie."

"Annie?" She raised her eyebrows.

He matter-of-factly, "Yes, my goat, and the mother of a new little batch of baby goats."

Goats she thought. How adorable was he?

As they soaked in the tub they spoke of many things. He told her about his siblings, a brother and a sister, both older. This was exactly the same for her. So, they were both babied and coddled, and got out of most chores. They laughed at that. He reached under the water and grabbed her by the ankles, gently pulling her closer to him.

When she got close enough he picked her up by the hips and set her in his lap. She wrapped her legs behind him in the tub. Feeling his excitement, she slowly lowered her self onto him, wrapping her arms around his neck.

He growled lowly with pleasure into her ear. She slowly began taking him in, with the water acting as an easy lubrication. He kissed her neck, again he hit the 'spot', he knew it well now.

He said, "Let's get out of here and I'll take you to a spectacular place."

He got out, fully erect, got a robe for her, fluffy and white, then put one on himself. He took her by the hand, and up a short stairway from the bedroom.

The new room was lit brightly by the moonlight coming through the windows in the roof. They could hear the wind howling. He laid her down on a large bed under the windows. Spending time kissing and whispering to one another, slowly feeling each other's bodies, he found his way with his hand to her still wet pussy. He began to rub her slowly, she, closing her eyes with a moan. He thumbed her clit until she began to squirm under his touch. She reached down and put her hand over his, encouraging his hand to go deeper and faster, raising her hips to meet his hand. Then with his arms around her waist, he slid to the side and turned her over. With her lying on her stomach, he got off the bed and slowly pulled her to the edge, feet on the floor, leaving her hands on the bed, he spat into his hand, and gently, eased his way into her ass, slowly, so as not to hurt her.

She had done this only a few times for her husband, enjoying the feeling inside, but having a hard time getting past the initial pain. Hurting a bit but wanting to please Peter, she finally felt him completely inside her, a delicious ticklish feeling.

He started thrusting slowly, being trepidatious, until she said, "Harder, baby." He then thrust to his heart's content, four, five, six times and then let out a loud slow groan. He lay on the bed next to her catching his breath.

After a few minutes, she got up and retrieved their champagne from the bathroom down the little stairs. When she returned, he was sitting up against his pillow. He sipped his champagne. "If I forget to tell you, love, you are so beautiful, and your ass is so tight, I love it!"

She smiled, took a sip, and placed her glass on the bedside table, where stood a picture of his wife. She reached over and put the picture facing down. "Are we safe here? I mean no one will drop in on us, will they?"

Understanding her meaning, "No, she really doesn't like it here and would never drive here at night." After some moments of silence, he said, "It was the poem."

"What?" Elizabeth looked puzzled.

"The poem-that was my favorite gift. It's like you paid attention and really attempted to get to know me. Thank you."

There was a guitar leaning against the wall near the chair. After kissing her, he got up and got the guitar, with her admiring his thin, muscular, but aging body.

He sat with legs crossed on the bed, in the darkened room lit only by moonlight. The light bouncing off the rich wood of the guitar as he played, he softly sang "You Are So Beautiful".

After making love for hours, they slept in the nude, snuggled under the heavy blankets . She fell asleep thinking about Sarah, his wife. She was blonde, with curly hair. She also looked good for her age, but seemed bored with him. How could she be bored with this wonderful man?

The next morning, he woke her with a steaming cup of coffee and a kiss. She was grateful. Making love for hours during the night had worn her out. He said as he stood and walked to the curtains, flinging them open wide, with the sun shining in, "I have a great idea how we should spend this glorious morning. I want to take you sailing on my boat."

She had known he was an avid sailor so she felt as though she was in good hands when she agreed. He said, "The waters of the Atlantic are frigid this time of year. Let's dress warmly, love."

She began to realize that he felt good with her company. They could talk, not talk, and it was always comfortable. He wasn't the big star anymore, and she wasn't just a lonely housewife. They were friends, a couple.

20
Chapter

His home sat on the edge of a beautiful cliff, overlooking cold, crashing waves. She thought the surf was a bit choppy. She hoped he could handle it. Once she got dressed in layers and put her boots on, she came down the stairway to see him coming from the kitchen, picnic basket in hand.

"Ah, there you are. Are we ready to go?"

She nodded in agreement. As they walked down the natural stone footpath, with a big dip now and again, he reached out his hand to help steady her. She felt the brisk wind on her face. When they reached the boat, he put the basket in, and then offered her his hand to help her board, always the gentleman. He untied some ropes and threw some colored flotation devices in the back of the boat. It was a beautiful boat, preserved natural wood, three sails, and a 'cozy' little cabin in the hull. She asked him if he'd like her to help him as he was putting up the sails.

"No, no love, I want you to sit back and enjoy the ride, the sun, the wind."

He finished the third sail, and there was plenty of wind, so they were being pushed along at a good clip. Once he had everything in place, he took a seat next to the rudder so he could steer. He said, "Come on over here and join me, darling."

She had to hold on to various things as she made her way over as the boat rocked back and forth. They sat close and he put his arm around her, pulled her close and kissed her.

"This, this is Heaven." Later, as the wind picked up and became even colder, he dropped anchor and told her, "Let's go down below and enjoy our lunch".

She was ready for that-she could barely feel her toes and her gloves were no longer keeping her hands warm.

They crept down the little stairway, ducking so as not to bump their heads on the low padded ceiling. He removed his puffy outer jacket and rubbed his hands together, in an effort, to warm them up.

"Shall we have a cup of tea? That should warm us up."

Unscrewing the lid on the large green metal thermos he had packed, he smiled. Elizabeth sat comfortably at the table as he unpacked the basket. He brought French bread, green olives-her favorite, grapes, prosciutto, hard cheese, and a slice of cheesecake for dessert. The basket was very elegant, and housed real china, silverware, and linen napkins. This was the way to do it, she thought.

As they dined, he would occasionally feed her, and she did the same. Gazing into each other's eyes, smiling, Peter tilting his head as he looked at her, taking in her features.

"I am having a really good time," Elizabeth said. "You really know your way around a boat, and I'm impressed."

"Don't be," he said. "I have fallen off my boat, more than once."

She laughed and said, "I hope not today."

As they re-packed the basket, full and warm from the tea, he said, "Now to fishing."

"Fishing?" she said with raised eyebrows.

"Yes, you know how to fish don't you?"

"As a matter-of-fact I do, and it was I, not my husband, who taught our daughter to fish, on Catalina Island off the coast of California." But, she explained, not before their bait, which they had bought off a vendor on the pier, was quickly swooped up by a seagull the minute they turned their backs to cast out! "Lesson learned for both of us."

He chuckled and smiled. "Well, we have live worms. They are good for many types of fish."

"Oh," she frowned, "I draw the line at baiting a hook with a live worm. Really, Peter, you will have to do that part."

"Ah," nodding, "my wife won't do it either, but the girls are OK with it."

A snippet into his family life, and she noted this time she didn't feel any jealousy, just casually listening.

They caught three fish, all of them Pink Salmon, and illegal to have where they were. They took their chances and put them in the cooler anyway.

When it was approaching one p.m., he said, "Let's bring this bugger home."

She watched from across the boat, his taking command of the vessel, clearly enjoying what he was doing. She felt pride, and was thankful for being a part of his life. Forget that he was famous, forget he was wealthy. To her he was just Peter now.

"Well I need to get going," she said as she stepped into her room to pack.

"You know I would be OK with you staying and meeting my daughter," he said.

Kissing him, she replied, "I appreciate you saying that, but it's not good, not practical."

His phone rang from inside his pocket. Sitting on the bed watching her pack he answered it. "Hello Sarah, love. How have you been? Or better, where have you been? Ah, OK, so how is Kevin?" He sat playing with the fringe on Elizabeth's pink scarf that was lying on the bed.

"Well, good for you, dear. You will be great in it I know. And when is it opening? Hmmm, I think I will be on set in Venice."

"We start shooting the week before, so I may have to miss the opening. Oh, I just got back from a quick sail -yes, yes, very cold, but the sun is shining and I am in a good mood ."

Elizabeth, rolling up a pair of jeans, looked up at him. He smiled and winked at her.

"Samantha phoned. She's joining me for tea this afternoon, and it'll be good to catch up with her. So, are you coming to Wales, love? I shall be here another two weeks, then off to Venice for some pre-production stuff and photo shoots, the usual."

It was weird, Elizabeth thought as she folded her sweaters. Acting was his job. He had to go to work like everyone, and be told what to do. The pedestal she had put him on didn't seem to have room for these types of routine chores.

"I know you don't like to be here, and yes, it is cold, but you also didn't want to go to Los Angeles because of the long flight. You know we need to do something together. People might start to talk, you know? OK, I love you too, darling. I will be in London in three days' time, just for the Cohen thing. OK, OK, I will. You too, bye."

He hung up while looking at Elizabeth. "I am going to miss you. I feel so free and uncomplicated with you. You don't demand anything of me, you are easygoing, I enjoy every minute I am with you." He took her hand. "Is this enough for you Elizabeth?"

She looked down at him, brushing his hair off his forehead. "It'll have to be." She smiled, leaned in and kissed him.

He grabbed her shoulders and pulled her to the bed, moving her luggage with his elbow. "Let me show you how I appreciate you." He slid his hands over her ass, kissing her longingly, softly. As they made love she could already feel how much she would miss him.

21
Chapter

The next morning in her hotel room, the ringing of her cell phone woke her. It was Peter calling. "Listen, I'm not ready to let you go. Don't fly out this morning." He asked her to stay in London, exlaining that in two days he was doing a show, a salute to Leonard Cohen. "I want you to come and see the show, and I really want you to join me at the after party," which would be taking place in a popular local social club she'd heard lots of good things about.

"What about Sarah?"

"She'll be at the show but she hates the after parties. She wont be there." He told her here would be dancing and dining, schmoozing and rubbing elbows with the famous. She agreed to stay, wanting to be there for him when he wanted her with him.

He phoned her hotel again later in the day and left a message for her. "I've put you on the list and I'll meet you there."

She spent the extra two days in London getting a feel for all of the sights, smells and sounds of the historical and lively city, and on her down time she made phone calls back home, taking on new tasks in her political woman's group, cajoling local leaders into supporting her candidate's bid for endorsement as Governor, and talking with her fellow committee members who were preparing for a floor fight at the state party convention coming up.

On the night of the party she was excited. After the show ended, she was incredibly proud of him. His singing had been fantastic and as always, he was quite the showman.

She taxied over to the club for the after-party, arriving a bit early, so she made her way to the bar for a glass of wine. She immediately recognized the who's who of the British acting world.

Sitting next to her at the bar, a young stud of a movie star, uber-famous, he was laughing with another guy and a girl. He at one point smiled and asked Elizabeth if she was enjoying herself.

Peter walked in about thirty minutes later, and to Elizabeth's surprise, with Sarah on his arm. Her heart immediately sank, out of fear and jealously, and anger from what she was not sure. Sarah was Peter's wife. Of course, she would be with him. Finding her place-marker at their table when dinner was being served, she smiled to everyone and took her seat.

The man sitting next to her, a Broadway producer she had heard of, introduced himself to her. "Have you met the others?" he asked.

Smiling, "Hello, I'm Elizabeth Wells."

The Producer asked, "Are you involved with the show, Elizabeth?"

"Oh, no. A few old friends invited me, and I am having a wonderful time."

He introduced her to Sarah, then to Peter, and another woman next to him, Peter's Publicist Janice Cameron. Then, thank God, the Cavalry showed up. Michael and James, the gay couple from the Wales dinner party. Rescuing her from idle conversation and from loneliness that was creeping in, she and Michael danced while others danced and mingled.

Eventually Peter found her on the dance floor and cut in on Michael. "I'm sorry, so sorry, love. She wanted to come.

I never would have placed you in this situation. She wants me to come back to the house in London. I'm sorry I can't see you tonight."

Elizabeth remained silent. When the song was over, Peter escorted her back to her seat. Seated at the table with Michael and Peter and his wife and the few others, he, sitting opposite her silently smoking a cigar with his hands perched in front of his mouth, not taking his eyes, and smoldering look from her, as she answered questions about her "freelance writing" and her political involvement and consulting for American candidates.

The wife was dressed in an emerald green dress and little black strapped shoes with a low heel. She looked lovely, although her hair left something to be desired.

She asked a question or two of Elizabeth making conversation. As Elizabeth answered her, she would take quick glances at him, seeing his smoldering sexy look behind the cigar smoke. She thought he had never looked sexier. She wanted to touch him.

She would return the courtesy of the conversation. She asked Sarah, "So which do you prefer, is stage or screen more fun to work on?"

A man, one of Peter's friends she had met earlier in the evening, approached their table and asked Elizabeth to dance. She was flattered, though she considered declining, but feeling a bit hurt by the turn of the night's events, she thought maybe this will make him a little jealous. As they danced she could feel his eyes on them, still staring over the top of his cigar. Her dance partner was handsome and she recognized him as an actor but couldn't recall his name or a specific movie he had been in.

He introduced himself as Charles. She thought he may have even been a Sherlock Holmes at one time. They chatted lightly about the play, the party, the weather, her stay in London. When the dance was finished and he returned her to her seat, thanking her for the dance, she noticed that Peter had turned sideways in his seat with his back to her, and was chatting with James, but he shot her a look. An unemotional but hard look, one she had never seen and couldn't read.

After dessert and coffee had been served, and as Peter saw her preparing to leave, he leaned over and told his wife he had to go to the men's room, he'd be right back.

Elizabeth rose to say her goodbyes, and told Sarah, James, Michael, Janice, the producer, and the others it was nice to meet them and that she hoped to see them again, then she made her way through the crowd near the door. As she descended the concrete steps of the trendy club, there was Peter, leaning against a tree waiting for her.

Grabbing her arm firmly, startling her, he said, "Please don't ever do that again. It's bad enough I know you have a husband I have to compete with." He hailed a limo, and opened the door for her. She was taken aback by his brusqueness. She frowned at him.

"I am really sorry, love, but I can't help it." She smiled to cover her concern, he leaned in and gave her a long and passionate kiss.

"Goodnight, darling."

She realized that this was the first time he had ever spoken to her that way and that she really was jealous of his wife being with him tonight.

She would be going home with him, sleeping with him, possibly having sex, waking and reading the morning paper with him. Elizabeth realized she wanted this. She had never acknowledged this to herself before, as she had always promised to herself that she would never hurt her husband in this way, and meant it. But she had to admit at least to herself, she had wondered what it would be like to be his wife, and be together more often.

She never knew that a seemingly innocent sexual tryst would turn into her falling for him, and he with her it appeared.

It hurt. She was jealous and it hurt. They were feelings unfamiliar to her and she wasn't sure how to handle them .

She would fly out around noon the next day. Getting up and out early, although he phoned her, she feigned being too busy traveling to reply, when in fact she was dying to speak to him, but still a bit hurt about last night.

22

Chapter

Elizabeth was walking precincts with a candidate she was supporting and advising in the next city council election, enjoying the sunshine and the exercise, happy to be home after four days in the UK.

This weekend would be Homecoming at the University. With Garrett preparing for the 'big game' against the school's worst rival, working long hours, he was starting to feel the exhaustion, but Elizabeth tried to pamper him as best she could, special meals, and back rubs. She was also excited to be going to Homecoming over the weekend, her Alma Mater, always a good time with old friends, nail-biting football games, etc.

This morning, preparing to go into work early, Garrett tried not to wake her, but hearing him stir, she got up with him, showered with him, getting romantic but not sexual. She quickly dressed and headed downstairs to prepare him a hearty breakfast.

She kissed him goodbye and reminded him the whole school and all its alumni were counting on him, "But no worries," she said with a wink and a smile. She went back upstairs and applied her makeup, expecting to tackle a large to - do list for the day.

Being a delegate at the upcoming State Republican Convention, amid rumors about challenges to proposed Rules

Committee changes, Elizabeth continued the swaying of party members over lunches and cocktail receptions. Her days were once again very full and exciting for her, but there wasn't a day that went by that he was not in her thoughts.

To her shock and surprise, he had been waiting for her husband to leave that morning. When Garrett was safely away, there was a knock at the door. As she took the stairs two by two thinking, "Who in the world?", she was floored when she opened the door to see the actor standing there. She hadn't even known he was in America.

He said, "I'm sorry about the after party. I want to take you on a date, on my motorcycle," as he thrust a helmet toward her.

"What, I... I can't believe you're here." Concerned that her husband might return home or lingering too long the neighbors may see them, she ran in the house, grabbed a light jacket, locked the door, and said, "Let's go."

They took a long, leisurely drive up to the Hollywood sign, then through Mulholland Canyon to the beach in Malibu, all the while her arms wrapped firmly around him. She, feeling special that he was sharing another of his passions with her.

Later they attended one of his movies together at a theater in Century City, a movie that had just opened that she had wanted to see. He said he wanted to view it with an audience that didn't know he was there, to hear and see their reactions. There was a heavy love-making scene in it, and Elizabeth felt a little jealousy creep up as she watched it, but then she reminded herself that after the movie he was going home with her. Not exactly home, but the Beverly Hills Hotel.

Growing up in L.A. when she and her friends were old enough to drive, they would cruise Beverly Hills hoping to catch glimpses of celebrities. Once they had snuck into the Beverly Hills Hotel and hung out by the pool.

This time she entered through the front door, with a famous actor, although they wouldn't know it by the hat and glasses he was wearing-James Bond strikes again.

They went to the shops inside the hotel and purchased bathing suits and flip flops, and watched the sun go down from the pool deck. Breaking the peaceful silence, her cell phone rang. It was Garrett, wanting to know what time dinner would be.

"I'm not cooking tonight," looking up at Peter, "not tonight," she said. "I'm tied up with paperwork at headquarters. I'll be home late. There are some good meals left in the freezer in the plastic containers, in fact, I left the last meat loaf for you. Heat it up, it'll be good. OK, honey, I'll see you later."

She knew she could not stay the night with Peter this time, so they remained poolside as the night lighting came on and the deck began to fill up with people stopping by for drinks.

The pool was lit up a beautiful aqua-blue color, and the palm trees were lit as well with tiny white lights, Elizabeth thought it was magical. They enjoyed each other's company, sipping wine and enjoying kissing and cuddling in one of the cabanas, until they both knew it was time for her to go. She didn't want to leave him, especially knowing he would be flying back to Heathrow in the morning. They said their long goodbyes, she with a bit of a tear in her eyes, but she was thankful to have had the day with him.

Their team won the Homecoming game. Garrett was all smiles, getting lots of congratulations, back slaps and handshakes. She felt proud of him and enjoyed seeing him revel in his success. Enjoying the friends and colleagues, the lovely buffet dinner provided by the university, for the coaching staff, players, and families. As the evening wore on, the lights came down, and couples began dancing.

Garrett stood up and extended his hand. "Elizabeth, may I have this dance?"

Smiling, Elizabeth said, "I thought you'd never ask."

Holding her close, he, looking into her eyes, she said,

"You know, Garrett, I am so very proud of you. You came from nothing and you have achieved and created all of this, and now some schools are talking Head Coach. You are my hero."

"I love you, Elizabeth." He kissed her.

"I love you, too," she smiled.

"Elizabeth, are you happy?"

A question she had not anticipated, but the answer came easily, "Yes, I am," and it was true. Of course , the various layers of that answer were lost on him, but he seemed satisfied with the answer.

The President of the University took to the stage to congratulate the team, and after thanking the head coach he further said, "I also want to say a few words about our Quarterbacks Coach, Garrett Wells. He has coached a terrific stable of Quarterbacks this year, and I wanted to be the first to let everyone know that our starting Quarterback Steve Landers, has just been announced as one of the five finalists for the Heisman Trophy this year. Garrett, come on up and say a few words," to whoops and hollers, and ' we love you coach', his players rising to give him a standing ovation, he took the stage.

"OK, you knuckleheads, have a seat. I just want to say that I love these guys, each and every one of them.

I enjoy coaching more than anything, and I am honored to be working with such a talented and classy group of young men. Steven, congratulations buddy, you deserve it. As Captain of the team you are an outstanding young man. You give back to your community, you set a good example, and I'm really proud of you. We are all pulling for you, kid."

On cue, the marching band struck up the fight song as the cheerleaders took over the dance floor with their routines .

23
Chapter

Tonight, the festivities were at her house. It had been a while since Elizabeth had the time to gather up her crazy girls. They were getting together for Corinna's birthday and a game of Bunco. It was just what Elizabeth needed, a night off -from everything.

After presenting Corinna with her cake and gifts, as they all settled in around the dining table, setting up the Bunco game, talk turned to men as usual, specifically this time about Elizabeth and Peter.

"What? Are you serious, you are going to tell us who it is? Do tell," said Karen straightening in her chair.

"Who was it, Elizabeth? Oh my God! Is it anyone we know? OK, wait a minute, we all need a refill," said Anna, standing to fill everyone's wine glass.

"Well, I can tell you this," smiling, "it was -Wonderful!! I am not ready to tell you who yet, but it was one of the best things I have ever done for myself."

Karen said, "That's not fair. You have to tell us who."

Elizabeth, lying, "You don't know him, so it doesn't matter."

"I know, it's someone in her political world," Laura piped in. "God, so many of those guys are so handsome and distinguished, and though they seem boring they are probably wild in bed, am I, right?"

"Let's just say he got me to try things I have never done before." Elizabeth smiled broadly with a little blush to her cheeks.

Jessica asked, "How many times have you slept with him?"

Three times," she lied.

Laura, said "OK...OK, start from the beginning."

"Well, the first time was easy and romantic, fun, and very physical. I never thought a first time with someone could be so fulfilling." Elizabeth smiled at the thought.

"So, how was he?" asked Jessica.

"Hmmm, where to start? Toying with them. "Well, he is hung!" Squeals of laughter and delight came from the group.

"Ah yes, Elizabeth, but did he know how to use it?" said the normally reserved Corinna, to more squealing.

"Honey, he wrote the book!" she said, laughing.

"Ahhhhh, you, lucky bitch," Anna said in mock jealousy. "So, did you do 'everything'?"

Elizabeth, knowing she was egging them on "Everything and more."

"Have you seen him since?" Karen pressed.

"Often," Elizabeth said with a sly grin.

"Oohh… la… la, he liked what you gave him the first time," Corinna laughed.

"So, are you guys like a couple?" Anna asked.

"Who cares, I want to know what new 'things' he had her try!" Mel said.

"You would Mel!" They all laughed. "Out of everyone at this table you are the one who would ask, aren't you?" said Elizabeth, throwing her cocktail napkin at her.

"I made you blush-do tell!" Mel laughing.

A slow smile developing, Elizabeth revealed, "Anal beads."

"What? Oh my God, are you serious?" Karen leaned in. "Well?"

"My orgasm blew my fucking mind. Most surreal experience of my life, and then I returned the favor," Elizabeth smiled devilishly.

"Whoo-hooo! You go girl!" Whistles and gasps all around.

"Are you going to continue seeing him?" Anna wanted to know.

"I want to but there is no future in it. I love Garrett and he loves his wife. We are just having some fun with one another."

"Who would have thought that you'd be the sneaky one?"

"Hey, a woman has to do what a woman has to do. I told you guys that Garrett and I were having some difficulties in that area. I think I just needed something new from someone new." Elizabeth was being completely honest.

"Well, you are my new hero. You had the guts to do it," said Karen.

"There is nothing heroic about it. I cheated on my husband, guys, but I just think you have to know yourself and listen to your needs, what helps you live, thrive."

Elizabeth held her glass up to cheer with the others.

"Here, Here!" Jessica joined in.

24
Chapter

Peter had arranged for a flight for Elizabeth to meet him in Telluride, Colorado for a ski weekend. Another lie to Garrett: "Honey, I am needed in San Francisco, the party Chairman has called a meeting to strategize."

As Peter filled her in on the trip plans, Elizabeth mentioned, "You know, my friends think I'm going out of town too much. It's becoming obvious something is going on.

"Well, I don't think you should hang out with your girlfriends anymore. They put bad ideas and thoughts in your head."

"Peter! They are not threatening to you, and they are my lifeline." A little insulted that he was serious.

She knew how to ski but not terrifically. Peter, on the other hand, was an expert. She liked his fearless spirit and his need to push things to the edge in his life.

While they skied different runs for the afternoon, they met up at the lodge for rest and a hot cup of tea. She noticed he had a broad smile on his face most of the day. Was it the sun shining, the perfect powder, or as she hoped at least in some way he was happy to be there with her.

When they returned to their chalet, she tied him up with his scarf. All he could do was try to use his mouth to reach her breasts as she leaned over him. Some of her touches made him quiver, ticklish, she thought. It was exciting and frustrating to him all at the same time.

"Come up here. Give me your pussy," essentially asking her to sit on his face. He licked and sucked and bit at her. She could feel his long hard nose against her clit and it felt good. When she and her girlfriends would get together that was always a saying she would use to make the girls laugh," I love a guy with a big nose."

Elizabeth poured champagne on his belly button and licked up his stomach, his chest. She used him to satisfy herself, and then him.

Spent and tired, their cheeks both a bit sunburned, they napped, then went to a cozy rustic steakhouse for dinner.

Clomping along with their boots in the snow arm in arm, disguised by fluffy jackets and beanies, smoked -filled chimneys all around, groups of people walking down the simple town square among the shops and restaurants.

After they had ordered their meal, he asked her to dance, on a small dance floor near the fireplace, a romantic Sinatra tune playing softly in the background.

As they danced he became a bit agitated. "Look at all these men looking at you. Can't they see you are with me?"

Smiling, Elizabeth said, "Let them look. I am with you."

They continued to dance, he continuing to sulk. After dinner, they stopped at a bookstore. She told him she had really begun writing a book of her own, something she always felt she had in her but had until recently never put in the time to collect her thoughts into book form. She told him it was about some public policies of the United States.

Continuing the discussion in front of the fireplace when they returned to their chalet, they talked about politics in England, the current state of the House of Lords and the House of Commons, emerging trends in climate and immigration policies. They talked for hours into the night. He told her he was impressed and proud of her and offered his help in any way he could in getting it published. She declined, saying that this project was all hers and she wanted to sink or swim based on her own merits. Their relationship was never intended to be about their careers, or his connections.

Though it was late, they agreed to a tantric love-making session, and after hours of repeatedly bringing each other to the brink of pleasure, when she finally had to let herself go, it was so intense she made scratches with her fingernails across his back and shoulder blades.

When he climaxed shortly after, the loudest he had ever been, she knew his was just as intense.

Silently watching him sleep, his rhythmic breathing, his boyish good looks, his salt and pepper hair, longer than most men his age wear it, falling a bit down the side of his face.

As he slept on his stomach, head turned to the side, leather beaded necklace around his neck, she took in his thin frame with taut muscles in his biceps and his back.

She recalled, some things she had read online, comments about him. She wished people could know the real him. She still checked back on his website to see what was being written. She often went to chat forums to read the latest. As with any social media she would come across some scathing comments, usually about something he said, something politically-charged, or his shoot from the hip response to a question.

The negative comments about his acting were few and far between. Even those who didn't like him as a person had to admit that he was a good actor. He lived on the edge and knew he never wanted to be pigeon-holed, and once he had choices he liked choosing roles that made people think or turned practical thinking on its head. She missed that she wasn't around in his youth, his early years as an actor, the struggles, the triumphs, watching him learn his craft. For this she envied his wife who had been around from the start and perhaps why she remained. As she gently stroked his face, she wished that they could always be like this.

Returning to L.A. on a quick flight from Telluride, setting down the luggage in his penthouse suite at the Beverly Hills Hotel, Peter began nuzzling Elizabeth's neck, sliding his hands down toward her behind.

"I cannot stay, Peter. I have to go home tonight. He has a team awards brunch in the morning and I need to be there with him. He knows I am flying in tonight."

Peter spun on his heel quickly and pushed her down hard on the bed, pinning her arms down. He began kissing her hard and desperately. The heat was scary but it also turned her on. She felt his passion rising, then he roughly turned her over, unforgivingly pulling her pants down over her butt, unzipped his fly, and forced himself into her ass. She protested and let him know he was hurting her.

He growled into her ear, "This ass is mine. It belongs to me," as he continued his assault. Finishing, he rolled off to the side.

She jumped up, pulling her pants back up.

"What the hell is wrong with you? I have never refused you. Why so rough? You know I like it a bit rough, too, but that was uncalled for."

With venom in his voice, he said, "I just didn't want you to forget that even when you are with Garrett, you belong to me."

Not believing her ears, she countered, "No, actually Peter, I belong to me, and no one else!" She grabbed her purse and left him there, on the bed, pants down, alone.

Three days later would be Valentine's Day. She wasn't even sure she'd see him. She wasn't sure she wanted to. He phoned and told her he was still in L.A. would she meet him for a drink. He wanted to see her before he left town. Although still a bit rattled by the other night, she agreed to meet him at Dan Tanna's in West Hollywood that night.

As she sat sipping her Zinfandel, she noted he was late, and she hoped his mood was not going to be as dark as it was the other night.

The Maître d' approached her. "Excuse me, ma'am, are you Elizabeth Wells?

"Yes."

"Ma'am, there is a gentleman up front asking to speak with you." Oh God, she thought, what is this about? Fear crossed her mind when she thought for a moment that perhaps Garrett had followed her. She could see as she approached a very well-dressed man, with a hat...a driving hat...like a chauffeur.

"Hello Ma'am. I have been asked by Peter Ballantyne to take you to meet him.

"Why? Where is he?"

"LAX, ma'am."

"LAX, what the hell…OK," shaking her head, "Fine."

The Maître d' spoke, "Mr. Ballantyne has already taken care of your bill..." smirking.

"Ah, I see," thinking, OK, both of them are in on this little plan.

Arriving at LAX in luxury, and directly on the tarmac at the private air field, the stairs to a Lear Jet slowly folding out and down. Out walked Peter, in a tuxedo and with two glasses of champagne, Elizabeth looking up from the foot of the stairs.

"Join me, won't you?" he smiled.

Making her way to the top, he handed her a glass and said, "Here is to our first Valentine's Day together. " They touched glasses and he kissed her soft and lingering.

They stepped inside the plane. She said, "This is lovely, but why here?"

"I am whisking you off for a romantic evening tonight - in Paris. Dancing, and laughing, making love."

"Are you kidding me? I can't."

"Why not? Let's make it happen. I love you and I want to spend this glorious holiday with you and only you. Call him, and make an excuse, because we leave in ten minutes." This was the first time he had actually uttered the words 'I love you' to her. She was astounded.

Luckily for her, Garrett had apologized for missing Valentine's Day with a gigantic bouquet of roses, as he would be out of town for a football camp this weekend .

Peter went on, "Also, I have ordered a few dresses in your size. You have your pick of them."

Looking around the plane, Elizabeth was impressed. Top grain leather, and wood, televisions and captain's chairs.

They adjourned to the fully equipped bedroom for a talk and Peter started, "Sometimes when I feel I'm losing I get possessive. I'm sorry if I upset or hurt you," he said with a puppy dog look.

"Garrett is my husband and he always will be. This isn't a movie, Peter. I'm real and I have real feelings. I am not here just for your pleasure anymore. You knew where we stood, we both agreed to this lifestyle, now you want to go changing it." She glared at him with a serious look.

He threw the TV remote that was on the bed. She started, "Peter, I didn't expect to fall in love with you and yet I have." Her voice wavered. There it was. The truth. A truth she hadn't even wanted to admit to herself.

He broke down too, yelling with a catch in his voice, "Don't you see I love you, too, and I want to be with you always Elizabeth?" His anguish was real. Calming down he said "Listen, let's stop this. It's Valentine's Day, a day for lovers." She joined the mile-high club at 37,000 feet.

25
Chapter

Another Valentine's Day without him, God only knew where he was. Sarah knew of his infidelities and she had some of her own, but she couldn't deny it still hurt, and the new sting she felt when she thought about him falling in love with someone else.

Sarah had begun to suspect that he was seeing someone longer than a night or two. She knew he was busy with filming but he did seem to take more frequent quick trips out of town. Although she loved him, they had two children together and years of marriage, but she had given up on worrying about his fidelity. They both had hurt each other over the years. She had told him once, "I don't know what you do when we are apart. The only request I have is, do not bring home a disease to me or fall in love."

She herself had fallen for a theater director she had worked with on a few occasions, they had a brief affair, but she had invested more than sex in him, she fell in love.

Peter had found letters between them. He was very hurt as this person was also his friend and had been his director in the past, too. Over time the hurt eased and the affair fizzled out, but the damage was done.

Peter then felt that he had *carte blanche* to do as he pleased. Each knew they didn't want the other falling in love with someone else. She had read and seen stories about him with this actress or that women, but she chose to look the other way, taking her pleasures as they came as well. She had known him since they were both very young. She knew what he needed, his own space and to do things his way. There wasn't much stopping him anyway. But he was the father of her children and she did have a special place in her heart for him.

On nights like this, these thoughts brought her down, left her with tears in her eyes. She still loved him even though she thought occasionally about leaving him. But the previous threats he had made over the years about her leaving him and the threats of taking the kids had stayed with her. It frightened her.

He was a good father when he was available, which was sporadic. They lived comfortably with both being celebrities and making a good living. More and more these days she seemed to enjoy her alone time, much like he had their whole life together. She had taken a small apartment in Paris where she would jump on the Underground and head to for a few days or the weekend. Because of the nature of their relationship, Peter constantly accused her of seeing someone there.

He said he thought it might even be an old friend of theirs. It was not, but he made threats just the same.

Her daughters would come to Paris often. They shopped and laughed, enjoyed the coffee and cuisine. Now that she had a grandson, Sarah found herself always thinking about the baby, and spending way too much money on things she found that the baby just 'needed'.

She was proud of her two beautiful daughters. They had her eyes, and his height. The thinner one with brunette hair had studied architecture at the Sorbonne. She started slow but she was really making a name for herself in the field.

Sarah worried about her spreading herself too thin. She had a career, the baby, whose father she did not marry but juggled joint custody with him. Her girls had grown up with nannies about, there to help her anytime Sarah was working or needed a break, so she urged her daughter to do the same, even offering to pay for it. But Mackenzie was a strong 'independent' woman. She assured her mom that she could manage everything.

Her other daughter, Samantha, the more, spunky of the two, had studied acting at NYU in the U .S. She had been working even before college, modeling in print -ads, hair products, etc., aimed at the teenage market. Now she was auditioning for parts she thought she could pull off. So far, her parts had been small, but she was moving forward, earning her Screen Actors Guild membership, which allowed for her to be more easily employable and recognized as a professional.

She took tips from both parents about acting, but never wanted to use her parents' fame to gain access, using a 'stage' last name so she wouldn't be recognized right off. She was thin and blonde, outgoing to the point that sometimes she got involved with boys who were no good for her.

Her parents worried about her choices sometimes. She liked dating actors, many of them already famous or on the way up, and actors can have roving eyes, as Sarah well knew. There were many admirers and chances to stray. Samantha had her heart broken on more than one occasion, often coming home to spend little girl time with 'daddy', who would baby her and make her feel safe and loved and gave her anything she asked for. Sarah had guessed that this was his way of making up for the many absences when the girls were growing up.

Sarah had been in a few films, but was most famous as a stage actress, often playing the lead in many of the best plays of this generation. She was in Colombia now on a shoot, but they weren't filming today, these days when she wasn't working, she began to get more melancholy, and feel more alone.

26
Chapter

After their lovers' night in Paris, Peter flew them to his home near London. His wife was filming out of the country and he wanted to take Elizabeth horseback riding. The day was typically overcast and smelled of rain.

"Let me show you around."

She could tell he was excited, and found it quite charming. First, he took her to the sheep pen, pointing out and calling each one by name, she noting his massive property stretched out before them.

Next on to the grazing cattle. "I raise them for the meat, but I can never part with them. We haven't slaughtered one in over four years," Peter laughed. "They are like my babies."

They hiked further on, to the goats; black ones, brown ones, white ones, all traveling in a clump. "Do you remember Annie, in Wales?"

"I do." Elizabeth said shaking her head.

"Well, these guys are her first tribe. They are all grown up now. We use them as weed-eaters."

Interlacing his arm through hers, they walked on and came upon a large corral. "And here we keep the horses."

"How many do you have?"

"Here... four, Scout, Mags, Paddy and Kid. Do you know how to ride?"

"Well this may be your territory, mister, but I had a horse growing up, so I am not a complete novice."

"We'll see," as he nuzzled Elizabeth's nose with his. He saddled the horses up as they talked and Elizabeth brushed and petted them. When they were ready he assisted her in getting on, then he decided to show off.

Hitting all the jumps in the pen, professional in every way, as he finished and rode up to her, she said, "Of course your posture and jumping skills are unbelievable, but I think it's just your cute riding pants that are doing it for me!" She wiggled her eyebrows.

Peter smiled. "Come on," he nodded.

After an hour or so of riding with him pointing out his property and beautiful things found in and around it, they came to a tree with a large log lying at the base. He helped her down and took up a spot leaning against the log.

Elizabeth spoke, "This place is very beautiful, tranquil."

"Yeah, I come here to think often." After a few moments of silence, "Did you know I am a grandfather? My grandson is two."

She told him she suspected he might be after spotting him with his family in the square in Prague, one of his girls was pushing a baby stroller.

"I really need to make some time to see him. He is growing so fast, and I want our relationship to be special. His name is Connor. Maybe you can meet him one day. "

"I'd love that," jumping at any chance to see his tender side.

His cell phone rang and he answered it. "Sarah, how are you?" as he got up, walking a bit away from Elizabeth for the conversation.

"Yes-yes. No, I don't." Just within hearing distance Elizabeth overheard......

"BECAUSE I SAID I DON'T WANT YOU TO, SO YOU ARE NOT GOING TO. DO YOU UNDERSTAND ME? IF I FIND OUT HE WAS

ANYWHERE NEAR THE SET, I'LL BEAT THE SHIT OUT OF HIM. DO YOU HEAR ME, SARAH? I'M NOT BLOODY FUCKING AROUND WITH THIS ANYMORE. YOU WILL DO AS I SAY, UNDERSTOOOOD?" He slammed the phone shut.

Frozen, not believing his tone, Elizabeth decided to pretend she hadn't overheard him, all the while wondering what the hell that was all about.

Peter turned the episode completely off. "So how about some lunch up at the house?"

Racing each other back up toward the house, in full gallops, he hollered to her, "I'm impressed!"

Pulling up on the reins near the stable, as the hands came to take the horses, he said, "You do know how to ride."

"Ahhhh, I still have many secrets that you need to discover," she smiled.

"And I intend to discover every, last one of them."

As they casually dined and talked, her mind kept drifting back to the phone call. She really didn't like to see that side of him. Didn't even like that it existed. Midway through their lunch of salmon with capers, Capri vegetables and iced tea, Mackenzie, Peter's oldest, came into the dining room.

"Hi."

Peter rose to greet her. "Hello, darling. What a nice surprise. Please join us," gesturing to a chair.

Mac eyed Elizabeth. "This is Elizabeth Wells. She is an American Writer."

Mac was curious. It was unusual for her dad to have a writer to the house. "Finally kicking around ideas about writing my memoirs. What do you think?"

"Just don't embarrass me, Dad!"

Peter laughed "Ahh, I would never."

"I was looking for Mom. Is she home?"

"Oh, she's in Colombia, love. They have started shooting the second season of her Netflix show. She's gone for three weeks. Do you need anything?"

"No, nothing I can't handle."

Peter wiped his mouth with his linen napkin. "How's Connor today?"

"Good."

"You should bring him over next weekend. I miss him."

"OK, I will. Listen dad, I can't stay. I've got to run, but I'll talk to you later," leaning in for a quick hug. "It was nice meeting you, Elizabeth."

"Yes, you too, Mackenzie."

"Don't let him spill too many secrets in his memoirs," Mac said, smiling.

"OK, I promise," Elizabeth smiled.

After a few more bites, "You know, Peter, I'm not staying with you, not here."

He touched Elizabeth's hand. "I know, love, I already booked you a room in Kensington. And I've already put you on the guest list for the performance, but I want you with me backstage until it starts. Deal?"

"Of course!"

"But in the morning, let's do a bit of sightseeing, yes?"

"Sure, sounds fun," she said.

27
Chapter

Peter laughed at Elizabeth as she tried to get a Palace Guard to smile by standing tip-toed nearly nose to nose. Hopping on and off a double-decker tour bus, total tourists, they were having fun. "Do you know two months ago, I was at Windsor Castle by invitation of the Queen and Prince Charles? They threw a party to honor British actors. "

"And today, dressed the way you are, you couldn't even deliver flowers to the front door," Elizabeth poked fun at him.

When they entered Westminster Abbey Elizabeth was stunned and overwhelmed by its beauty. This was one place she and Kat hadn't had a chance to make it back to on their trip. She had seen most of the stuff in London on her other journey with Kat but she couldn't resist revisiting them because of his enthusiasm and his pride in sharing his homeland with her.

In the Abbey, with its beautiful architecture and history, Elizabeth discovered that 'Poets Corner' was her favorite part. They had tomb plaques for Jane Austen, The Bronte Sisters, Robert and Elizabeth Barrett Browning, Lord Byron, Geoffrey Chaucer, Lewis Carroll, Henry James, Noel Coward.

She was also pleased to see in a reverent location in the Abbey the plaque for Charles Dickens, her favorite Author.

She was further excited to see them for Sir Lawrence Olivier, Neville Chamberlain, Sir Winston Churchill, Sir Isaac Newton, everywhere she looked in the grand church, she saw evidence of Britain's greatness, as she recalled their works in her head.

Afterward, stopping for what Peter referred to as the "absolute bloody best fish 'n chips in London" at a curbside café, they relaxed, ordered ale and the fish n' chips, and he was right, they were the best she had ever tasted.

She noted that in England, the batter and oil were so much lighter than how they cooked them in the U.S., which usually made her feel sick, they were so heavy, but England knew what they were doing, and sprinkling a little malt vinegar always made it a new experience.

Rain threatened to come down, with a light fog rolling in now. It gave the city a completely different aura and caused Peter to pull Elizabeth close to him to help keep her warm.

"OK, love, are we ready to top off this lovely afternoon with a spot of tea or a nice Irish coffee?"

"That, my dear is an excellent idea." Elizabeth hugged him.

"Let's go to the Mayfair Hotel. They are cozy and their tea cakes fantastic."

"Lead the way tour guide."

Once inside the elegant hotel, they made their way to the tea room, and she decided an Irish coffee would suit her mood nicely. He ordered Earl Grey tea and a cake tray.

As they casually ate and drank, laughing about the day's events, she reminded him that she was leaving in two days.

"I know love, but I don't want to let you go."

She decided she had to broach a subject she had been mulling over. "Peter, what does all of this mean, us? What are we, where is it going, what do you want from me? Can we really go on just being-this?

I'm not saying I need more, but I just wonder what it all really means."

Setting his tea down and taking her hand, he responded, "Elizabeth, I know I love you, and as far as I am concerned I would be happy spending the rest of my life with you like this. I'm happy, are you?"

She smiled, "I'm happy with you, too, but I wonder if it's fair to Garrett-and Sarah, and ourselves. We are never going to be together in a permanent way. What about Christmases and special events in ours and our family's lives?

We cannot share those, and without hesitation I tell you I love Garrett, and as I told you from the start I never plan on leaving him. But what are we denying ourselves living this way? There are nights I want to be with you, just to hold you, or to make love to you. My birthday was wonderful with Garrett and the kids, but there was a small hole in the day that was meant to be filled with you."

"I feel exactly the same way, Elizabeth, but what are we to do?"

"I don't have the answers, Peter, for now only the questions. I don't know what to think-or feel."

Peter squeezed her hand with a direct look. "I would marry you if you got a divorce. It's not just lip service."

"Peter, I love you and I love Garrett too, and I don't want to leave him." She paused to let that sink in, then she sat up and brightened "You know what, we are having a lovely time. Let's not worry about all that now. This clotted cream is amazing."

He put a dot of whip cream on her nose. Smiling, he said, "You are amazing."

"I have a wonderful idea," Elizabeth said looking at him with a sexy leer and wiggling her eyebrows. "We have a bit of time left. Let's go upstairs, whatda ya say?"

"Why, Mrs. Wells, are you trying to seduce me?"

"Well-is it working?" wiggling her eyebrows again.

"You don't have to ask me twice, love. Let me go take care of it. Don't get away."

"What, and leave all these wonderful sweets behind? Not a chance!"

"I'll be right back."

As she watched him leaving the tea room she loved how he wore his jeans snug and tucked into his leather boots, very European and masculine, running his hand through his salt and pepper hair. She was glad he was getting a room. At that moment, she wanted him badly.

As she felt his tongue and lips, against her skin, her neck bending to ask for more, she wasn't sure what it was about this man, but she couldn't get enough of him touching her, with his mouth, his hands and his body. He did things to her she hadn't thought possible. As he kissed her neck while he was inside her, she could not even form words. She became like Jell-O in his arms.

Elizabeth arrived backstage the following night for his play in which he was playing a Civil War Era General, greying, with a full beard and a dark presence, ready to take the stage, to start foreboding about the war, and barking out orders. To Elizabeth's surprise, his daughter Samantha was in the dressing room with a famous young actor, when she arrived. Samantha was hugging her father.

"Oh, hello, Elizabeth." Peter to his daughter, "Honey, this is Elizabeth Wells."

"She is interviewing me for uh, an article for an American paper." Lying seemed to come easily to him now. Elizabeth wondered if he was always honest with her.

"Hi, I'm Samantha, and this is Christian."

"Hello, it's a pleasure to meet you both." His daughter was lovely and resembled both her mother and father. Thin and blonde, beautiful face, she was genuine, not phony, just like her father. Elizabeth immediately recognized her guest as a new young American actor, coming up after a small role in a superhero movie. Built well, dressed very well. He seemed a bit ill at ease. She was not sure if it was due to Peter's presence or if it was just the whole showbiz thing was still new to him. It didn't help that Peter had the beard and steely eyes. He could easily be an imposing, dark figure. No wonder the kid was scared, she thought.

"Well, Daddy, we just wanted to drop in to say hello. We'll let you get to your interview. By the way, Dad, are we all going to Wales for Christmas this year? I'd like to bring Christian if that's OK,"

He hugged her. "Yes, darling, whatever you want."

More jealousy, more pain for Elizabeth. He kissed her on the cheek and shook hands with Christian. "Don't talk so much lad," he smiled to him.

As the door closed behind them, Elizabeth wrapped her arms around Peter's neck, kissing him softly.

"Mmm-you smell and taste like your character's cigars from the matinee."

Peter returned the kiss and then backed a bit away. With a stern voice he said to her, "I called you three times last night Elizabeth. Where were you? Who were you with, what were you doing, Elizabeth?"

Surprised by his tone, and also affected by his imposing look, she responded, "When did you call?"

"Don't play silly games with me, Elizabeth!"

"What games, Peter? When did you call?"

"About seven."

"Oh, yes-I was at the hotel gym. Why didn't you leave a message?"

With the hard, steely look of his current character, he bore his skepticism in her eyes. "Hmmm", nodding his head.

Sitting in the airport waiting for her flight home, she picked up a copy of Entertainment Weekly Magazine that had been dis-carded on one of the seats. As she thumbed through it, she came to an article about the net wealth of some of the biggest Hollywood stars. Peter was 6th, with $245 million. She gasped. She had no idea.

Apparently, he owned restaurants, real estate, automobile collections, race horses, yet he really was just a simple guy. It didn't take much to make him happy, although it did explain the home in Wales and the house staff.

As she continued flipping through the magazine, she came to the page covered with little snapshots of the stars out and about. Stunned she came to one of them walking together. It was on their ski trip, and it was labeled, "Peter Ballantyne seen with an 'unidentified woman' in Telluride, Colorado.

She recognized herself by the bundle of clothes, scarf, and hat that she was wearing, but luckily felt that no one could truly tell who she was. Of course, this lit speculation that he was again seeing someone other than his wife, and this couldn't be good for either of them. She prayed that this wouldn't mean the press would start hounding him and trying to get to his dirty laundry. That could mean people following them, photographers in the bushes, neither of them wanted that. It could change the direction of their relationship in some way.

She noticed on this flight that each trip now felt shorter and shorter. Her mind began to drift as she reflected on how his personality seemed inconsistent. She began to wonder what the cause was.

Getting comfy at home, sitting in her window -seat, she opened her email, and Elizabeth was startled by the only new message in her inbox. It was from Sarah Cowen -Ballantyne. Unsettling to say the least.

Oh, God, she obviously knows, Elizabeth thought, letting out a long loud breath- "and here goes not thing."

"Elizabeth, Peter is not what he seems. He has made me a prisoner in our marriage. Over the years, we have had our showdowns, but it is his threats that have kept me from leaving. Threats to take my children away, fear of him getting physical. He calls the shots. I do not even have friends without his consent. He has told me he won't let anyone else have me.

I may have a public career, too, and from the outside it probably looks like it would be easy to leave, but that doesn't remove the fear of him

Why would she tell me this? If she believes we are seeing each other, shouldn't she hate me? Is this real? Elizabeth knew to some degree it was the truth, through his occasional weird behavior and the phone calls she had overheard Peter make to Sarah.

Do I respond, acknowledge that I read it? Should I tell Peter? How did she get my email address? The email created so many more questions than answers.

28
Chapter

Peter had been working very hard in the time that Elizabeth had known him. He had won many awards in his career and had begun receiving numerous 'Lifetime Achievement Awards', as is the nature in an aging actor's life. It had been many years, however, since his Academy Award win. So, the phone call he received in the middle of the night, shortly after the award nominees were announced in Los Angeles, was to tell him that a picture he had worked on the previous year, but released this year, had been nominated for Best Picture, and he for Best Actor.

He couldn't believe it. After all this time, was his work still good enough to receive awards of this caliber?

He rang Elizabeth at dawn L.A. time with excitement. "Love, guess what?"

"What, what is it?" She was in the kitchen, barely awake and fumbling to make a pot of coffee.

She was alarmed even though she could hear joy in his voice.

"I've been nominated for an Oscar, for "Richard II!"

"Oh my God, Peter, I am so happy for you and proud of you! You have worked very hard. You so deserve this," Elizabeth elated.

He said, "It's about fucking time." She thought that

sounded a bit ungrateful, but the laughter in his voice was just his joy seeping through. He said, "You know this will mean I actually have to work harder now, interviews, appearances, parties, politicking for votes. Although I enjoyed winning in the past, all of this jockeying is really annoying. "

"Well, do it for me," she said. "I didn't see you win the first one and I want to be filled with pride watching you on television accepting the next one."

With a smile in his voice, he said, "Well, there is another good side to this. I will be spending copious amounts of time in L.A."

Three days before the Oscar ceremony, Peter asked Elizabeth to meet him for lunch at the Chateau Marmont, a place they knew well. But it was a highly public place and a highly-publicized time in Hollywood. The lunch had to appear completely platonic, but he leaned in close, and whispered, "I have a surprise for you."

Raising her eyebrows, a broad smile on her face, she answered excitedly, "Tell me."

"I am taking you to the Oscars." A toothsome grin on his face.

"What? How?"

"Let me worry about that. Of course, Sarah and I are going together, but I want you there, too. Listen, when we are done with lunch, I want to take you shopping for something special to wear."

"Peter, are you serious?" Trying very hard not to touch him or appear too intimate. Spending the day shopping for her dress and jewelry all the while with him incognito. It felt exciting to be 'getting away' with something all day. Today she was part of his world. She enjoyed herself immensely. Trying on dresses for his approval, and because of the high -end nature of the shops, the store staff treated her exceptionally, making recommendations and offering wonderful compliments. She felt a bit like Julia Roberts in Pretty Woman.

She had finally decided on a sweeping silver dress that accented her breasts and minimized her waist and it looked radiant with her skin tone. Her astrology charts had always told her that grey and silver were her colors. Now she believed it. She felt beautiful in the pricy dress, for which he shelled out over $12,000. She tried to talk him into something cheaper, but he had said, "Nonsense, love. You look absolutely smashing in that dress. It's the one!"

Next on to the shoe department. She had to be careful to select a shoe that was sexy, but had a closed toe for her prosthetic. She selected a strappy, mid -size stiletto in black, with plenty of Swarovski bling. She would finally be as tall as he was.

She took the opportunity in the corner of the shoe department, to lean into him, planting a seductive kiss on his lips. Growling, he nuzzled her neck and ear. "You are so beautiful. Are you happy?"

Elizabeth smiled. "I am very happy, but not because of all this. I'm happy because I am here with you."

"I love you, Elizabeth Wells."

"I love you," she whispered, "Peter Ballantyne."

When it came to jewelry she wanted something simple, yet he insisted on a whole ensemble, necklace, earrings, and bracelet. While she would have been content with Swarovski, he insisted on the 'real' thing, plunking down the $32,000 on his black American Express Card. She truly felt like a princess. She was equally excited when he told her he had already arranged for her to get her hair, makeup and nails done on the morning of the Oscars by true Hollywood professionals. Now she looked forward to his winning the award. That would complete the fairy tale.

As a last-minute decision to check into the Hotel Marmont for a lazy afternoon of love -making was coming to an end, she asked him about his ring, the one he always wore, even in his movies. "What is the significance of that ring?"

"It belonged to my grandfather. When he passed, my grandmother gave it to me. She said, he always said I reminded him of himself. He was really my hero, he was kind, funny, and generous, I spent a lot of time with him when I was young, and he was really wonderful."

"You know you remind me a bit of my grandmother. She loved politics, had a feisty side, and when she cared, she cared deeply. But the ring really is one of my most prized possessions. I never take it off."

"It suits you," she said with a smile.

By late afternoon he was preparing to leave the hotel as he and his wife were expected at a Pre -Oscar dinner for presenters and nominees at the Beverly -Wilshire Hotel.

"Can I ask you a question, Elizabeth? You're not still sleeping with Garrett, are you?"

Cocking her head, thinking the question was bad timing, she replied, "He's my husband, Peter. Of course, I am."

Peter slowly shook his head up and down, not saying anything. After a long goodbye, she wished him all the luck and thanked him for the gifts.

It was hard to say goodbye. She knew he had to go back to the hotel with his wife and she had to go home to Garrett. Their day had been wonderful, but she anxiously looked forward to Oscar Night and to seeing him again.

Mid-morning, she arrived at the hotel suite at the Marmont he had reserved for her.

Shortly afterward her 'beauty team' arrived. She had her hair done by true Hollywood artists, who created an up -do that showed off her slender neck. Then they did her make -up. She felt stunning, and couldn't believe it was her looking back from the mirror.

In the afternoon, sitting in the back of the black, sleek SUV he had sent to pick her up for the Oscars, her mind began to drift to Sarah's email.

She hadn't decided yet whether to tell Peter about it.

She wasn't sure what she was going to do, confront him, let it slide, talk with Sarah about it. She wouldn't have to decide today, but she knew after the excitement and attention of the Oscars, she had to make a decision.

She was dropped off at an entrance for those invited but not famous guests, but not before taking in the chaotic and exciting scene outside the venue. The limos came in three -deep on the road in front of the site which had been closed for the event. Black limos of all shapes and sizes, utterly elegant people stepping from them, perfectly quaffed hair, crisp clean outfits, and sparkling jewelry.

Crowds filled the bleachers on either side of the red carpet, screaming when crowd favorites arrived, some of them honoring the fans by stepping over to give an autograph or take a photo with them. The celebrities made their way through the maze of media outlets set up along the red carpet poised to get the interview, to find out who they were wearing or asking nominees what they thought their chances of winning were. Intense excitement, glamour and flash bulbs, on this, Hollywood's most celebrated night.

Once inside the theater Elizabeth was shown to her seat. Peter had gotten her a single ticket, near the stage, but a bit away from where he and Sarah were to sit, a hard ticket to get but assuming because of his nomination he was able to swing it.

Elizabeth scanned the room, she spotted Meryl Streep, Sandra Bullock, and Sally Field in the second row, Leonardo de Caprio nearby, never one of her favorites.

Generally, in every direction she looked, she saw a celebrity. Usually celebrities were not of much interest to her, but this room was filled with mega stars, and it was quite overwhelming to her. First the disbelief that after so many years watching it on television, that she was there in person and a guest of one of the megastars, whom she happened to be sleeping with.

She saw them enter the room, Peter and Sarah. She had her arm through his, smiling, as they made their way to their seats, shaking hands and greeting many of their friends. He was handsome in his white tuxedo jacket, with a Nehru collar, and she in a sapphire-colored gown with a V-neck studded in diamonds. Quite lovely, Elizabeth thought, and she could see she'd had her hair done but, yet again, they missed the mark and her 'do' looked like it was just a pile on her head. Meow, she thought. Be nice.

Elizabeth was thinking that it should be her sitting there with him, saying hello to everyone. She was the one who was in love with him and she wanted the world to know. After they were seated, Peter sought her out, with a smile upon seeing her.

The show opened to a headlining top comedienne with her own show on television. Her dry and sarcastic sense of humor had the room in stitches from the beginning. Her raunchy innuendos and comments about this year's nominated movies and stars kept everyone laughing and in a good mood for the three-hour long show.

Seeing Peter presenting an award on stage, Elizabeth smiled a knowing smile to herself. There he is, she thought, in all his glory, and she loved him.

When finally, toward the end of the show Peter's category came up, and they began to show clips and a live shot of the other nominees, for the first-time Elizabeth worried that he might not win. The competition was fierce. All the nominees had given stellar performances.

As they showed his clip and panned to him in the audience, he smiled graciously into the cameras. Elizabeth feeling nauseous suddenly, so nervous for him. The actor and actress presenting the award, trying to be funny with pre - written witty banter, finally uttered the words

"And the Academy Award goes to-" in unison, "Peter Ballantyne for Richard II!"

Oh, my God…it's him, it's him! She felt elation. A tear began to trickle down her face. Dabbing at it with a tissue, she waited with bated breath to hear him speak.

In his tall elegance, he climbed the stairs. Taking his statue in hand, "Wow, this is really wonderful. I-I really can't believe it. I figured I was too old to win another Academy Award."

He set the statue on the podium and pulled out a short list from his jacket pocket and laid it on the podium.

"I would like to thank…," he read a brief laundry list of agents, reps, and publicists, "my wife for always standing with me, and I would like to thank others, you know who you are," he said as he looked in her direction and turned the ring on his finger that they had just talked about in the hotel the day before.

She knew exactly who he meant. Her heart melted. He was thinking about her during one of the most triumphant events of his life.

After attending the Post-Oscar Governor's Ball with Sarah, Peter dropped his wife at their hotel, he had been invited back to Rex Masterson's house with the boys.

He was enjoying his occasional pleasure of smoking cigars, drinking whiskey, lounging, and long discussions with his old friends. Many of them were also famous actors, and many he had known since starting his career more than forty years before.

Rex and Peter were reminiscing about the Playboy Mansion parties of years ago, "do you remember the 'anything goes' feeling of those times? Cocaine, marijuana, sex with not quite legal girls, drinking into oblivion sometimes for days. Ah, those were the days. Everyone has gotten so uptight!" Rex delighted in his memories.

Ballantyne chuckled. "Yeah, those were some fun times. I'm too old for that crap now."

"Well, I'm not and never will be," Rex smiled with a devilish toothsome grin he was most famous for.

"Have you heard about this thing called the deep web or the black web?" Rex asked as he took a puff from his fat cigar.

"No, what's that about, mate?" Peter said as he loosened his bow tie.

"I discovered it about a year ago. Let's just say anything you could ever possibly want can be found there."

"Ahh, and what exactly are you looking for there?" Peter asked, pointing at him with his thinner cigar between his index and middle finger.

"Young ladies, of course." Rex smiled as he took a giant gulp of his whiskey.

"As in not yet eighteen-year-old ladies?" Peter shot him a sideways glance.

"You got it, old friend. It's an addiction," Rex admitted.

"Well, you've been pretty lucky over the years, but you better be careful. One of these days one of those girls is going to bite back and you'll be living with Polanski," Peter admonished.

"Nah", again with the smile, "they love me," Rex puffing his cigar.

Waking with a hangover, Peter vaguely remembered how he got back to the hotel. He remembered why he didn't get together with Rex as often anymore. He was hard to keep up with and he could always drink Peter under the table. Also, Peter had given up the wild skirt chasing and carousing of his younger days.

Sitting in front of his computer at the desk in their palatial suite, not ready to have the curtains open yet, hunched over, drinking his coffee and checking his email, last night's discussion surfaced in his hazy brain. 'Deep Web'. Was Rex serious about that?

Always thirsty for knowledge, he decided he would investigate when he returned home after their flight, which was leaving in a few hours.

Peter rang Elizabeth, "Good morning, love. How are you doing? We're flying out in a few hours. I feel like hell. I got drunk with Rex last night, and boy am I feeling it today."

Elizabeth laughed. "You are not a young, spry frat boy, Peter. You should know better. But I'm sure you had a good time, and Peter, congratulations. I am so very proud of you."

"Thank you, love. That means a lot."

"Hey, have you ever heard of this thing called the deep web, or black web?" Peter inquired.

"I have, Kat told me about it once. Basically , it's a black market. Anything, well- not legal can be found there, apparently. Why do you ask?"

"Oh, Rex was spouting off about it. I wasn't sure I even believed him. So, love, I must go. I'll call you tomorrow when I get home. I love you Elizabeth."

"Isn't she there with you?" Elizabeth worried he might be overheard.

"She's in the shower." He looked over his shoulder to make sure.

"Be careful. I love you, too. Have a safe flight Academy Award Winning Movie Star" she laughed.

29
Chapter

Back in Wales, alone in his library, Peter decided to access this 'deep web' for the first time. After a half an hour of searching, he thought, this place is like a desert, flat and no trails leading to anywhere. Is this a scam?

After more fishing around he found an index, which had him tunneling through website after website, he came across a synopsis about how it worked. He discovered it was untraceable, using straw ip addresses. As he began opening ads, he sensed that some of them were scams. Also noting the high prices, he guessed that only natural for such high stakes requests. Rex was right- you can get anything here.

The library door creaked open. "Hi Dad."

"Hey, Mac," surprised to see his daughter.

As she neared the desk she saw that he was on the deep web.

"Dad, what are you doing?"

"Oh, a friend told me about this and what you can buy, see, and do on this deep web thing. I wanted to see if it really exists-and it seems to."

"Dad, really, you should not be messing with those sites. They are seriously bad news, full of people you don't ever want to mess with."

"OK, OK." He put his hands up. "I was just a bit curious."

Peter's cell phone rang. Picking it up, he recognized Elizabeth's number.

"Have a seat Mac, I have to take this."

"Hello, yes, hello, how are you? Nice to hear from you."

Elizabeth, sensing something was off, asked, "Are you alone?"

"No-actually I'm not."

"Do you want me to call back?" knowing now her call was bad timing.

"No, no. That's OK. So, when are you leaving for your conference? This Friday? Uhh-huh. How long has he been gone? I see. So, you're both coming home on Sunday? Oh, I don't know. I was thinking I might pop by, say hello . Next week then, I guess. Well, I wish you the best of luck with your battle. I know how much you enjoy the process. You will be in heaven."

Elizabeth, sensing the person in the room with him, said, "OK sweetie, I'll let you go. I'll call soon."

"All right, thank you so much for calling."

Peter turned to Mackenzie. "So, what brings my lovely daughter to this stuffy old room?"

"I've got a new commission- to design a small theater in Dublin. I thought that would make you happy."

"You're right, it does! Fantastic!" He smiled and gave her a high-five.

30
Chapter

"Hey coach, I saw Mrs. Wells at LAX when I was flying back from visiting my folks a couple of weeks ago. I was too far away to say hi, though."

"Oh, cool…a few weeks ago, you say?"

"Yeah, a few Monday's ago. I made a quick trip home for the weekend, it was my Mom's birthday, I wanted to surprise her."

"Good for you, I bet you made her happy. Your squad is waiting for you, bud, get out there."

"OK, coach." The player sprinted off with his helmet in hand.

Monday-Monday. Garrett had originally suspected she might be sleeping with a younger man, and because of the status of their lack of love making he really couldn't blame her. She had attended a lot of political functions and meetings in the past, but they seemed to be more frequent now, and for more days. This was why he was not totally surprised by the letter he received. And now the player's comments were just re-confirmation of something he already knew. Elizabeth had lied about that weekend. Again.

He had already started penning a letter to her; he hadn't had the heart to finish it.

"I think you thought it would be fairly innocent, and didn't know you would get caught up in it all. You fell in love with him, but regardless

I want to be with you. I don't think we should throw away the years, our memories, and the past." The letter went on, *"Elizabeth, you should have thought about us before you let all this happen."* Oh God, had he lost her for good? He thought as he wrote, *"I pray you stop seeing Ballantyne."* He was sure that she didn't know that he knew, or that he already knew who it was.

Their love had changed over the years, and sex had become an event, only being able to perform with Viagra, and he also couldn't seem to bring her to orgasm anymore. It had all become not worth it for him. But God, he still loved her, and did not want to lose her.

Kat was home for the weekend so her mom treated her to lunch. After all the dish about school and her friends , Kat asked Elizabeth, "Have you heard from Peter lately? Do you love him, Mom?"

Initially she was hesitant to talk about this with Kat. They never talked about Peter.

She didn't want to make her weekend home awkward, but she decided her daughter was a young adult and deserved an honest answer. She looked at Kat a minute without answering.

"I do, Kat, I do."

"So, what about you and Daddy?" touching Elizabeth's hand.

"I also love your father. It's possible to love two men, but I will forever be with your father. He is the father of my children. I have lifelong memories with him, the ups and downs. He is a good man, Kat, and I will always love him.

"So, then, what about Peter?"

"Well, I will continue to love him as well, but we both know that we will never really be together more than we are now, and for now it works for us."

"Is it hard to be away from him?" Kat feeling for her mother's predicament.

Elizabeth shook her head. "Sometimes, but I know I'll see him soon enough, so I just go on with my life until then."

31
Chapter

Elizabeth heard her name being paged at the San Diego Marriott where she was actually in town for a political conference, no lying this time. She found the nearest house phone. "Yes, this is Elizabeth Wells, I was just paged."

The front desk informed her that she had a visitor. She was perplexed, wondering if it was the candidate. She made her way from the meeting room to the front lobby. There in a black t-shirt, a Yankees baseball cap, fitted blue jeans, and sunglasses stood Peter Ballantyne.

"What are you doing here?" she smiled.

Peter smiled broadly. "Well, here you are in a hotel with lots of men."

Elizabeth was not amused. "Really, Peter, is it me you don't trust?"

He walked up to her. "Well, you have heard if they cheat with you, they'll cheat on you." He winked at her.

Squinting her eyes in disbelief, Elizabeth responded, "I could say the same thing. You think you'd know me well enough by now to know that is not me. I am with you, Peter, because I fell in love with you. I already have more than I can handle. I'm not looking for more. You can't just show up trying to control every situation."

"I want to know what you do when I am not around, who do you see, where do you go?" Peter searching her eyes.

"Peter that is interrogation-and it's suffocating."

In her hotel room, as she came out of the bathroom, Peter gazed at her. "You are so cute in your little business suit, your hair up and all business, the glasses, you look like a formidable opponent, and you are driving me crazy. Unpin your hair. I want to see it fall to your shoulders."

"I don't want to have sex with you. I'm mad at you for not trusting me." She slipped off her heels.

"It's just who I am Elizabeth" he said, as he slid his arms around her waist.

"Well, it's not OK," she said to him with a serious face.

"Come on," he whispered. "You know you want to have sex with me."

"Do I?" she glared at him.

A devilish smile crossed his face. "Look me in the eye and tell me you don't."

Looking him in the eye, a smile spreading across her face. "I can't say no to that face."

"Ah ha!" He picked her up and twirled her around.

Sitting naked on his lap, legs wrapped around the chair, he naked and hard, she took him in, controlling him and maximizing the depth, while he concentrated on kissing 'the spot' on her neck, bringing her to a quick and soft orgasm. Then he grabbed her ass and thighs hard, holding her in place as he rammed himself into her three then four times not taking his eyes off of hers. He wanted to look at her as he pounded her, the look of ecstasy on her face. Climaxing, he collapsed into her breasts, beads of sweat on his forehead. She grabbed handfuls of his sweaty hair.

Afterward, she showered and then reapplied her make - up. From the bathroom, she overheard the call he was making to his wife.

"I don't give a shit, Sarah, who else is going to be there. You are not going!"

He really can be mean, Elizabeth acknowledged to herself.

"You have to leave. Today. I have work to do." She looked at him poignantly.

"I am having dinner with my agent later then I'm flying home, but Elizabeth, you have to answer my phone calls. All sorts of thoughts crop up in my head when you don't respond. But I really want to stay and see you in action."

"You can't, it's a closed session."

He narrowed his eyes. "Closed? Closed to Peter Ballantyne?"

"Especially to Peter Ballantyne." She kissed his nose.

"So, are you going to get your candidate for Governor nominated? How's that going?" Peter asked interested.

"Actually, it's looking very good." She reached in the closet for her suit jacket. "But this weekend is about hospitality suites, and handholding and convincing the remaining few holdouts for the votes we still need, to me the most fun part of the process."

"And exactly how much are you willing to give, to put on the line?"

"Honestly, Peter!" He was trying to joke but she knew there existed a modicum of truth to his comment.

"Hey, by the way, I got a script I'm reading. They want me to play the Secretary of Defense. The writing is a bit dry, but the story is fantastic."

"I'd love to read it," said Elizabeth with interest.

"Let me decide if I am going to take the part first."

"Peter, what would you say if I said I was considering running for office myself? Perhaps State Assembly or State Senate? Garrett thinks it's a great idea. I would have the party backing."

Putting his arms around her from behind, looking at her in the mirror, he exclaimed, "I would be very proud of you - but that would mean that there will be people snooping into your-our private lives. We'd have to be even more careful."

"I don't know, I'm just kicking the idea around." She turned to kiss him.

32
Chapter

Tap dancing, swerving past one another while preparing dinner, Elizabeth and Garrett laughed and finally came together to enjoy a meal and discuss their upcoming plans.

Garrett started off, "So our first game in the playoffs is tomorrow at seven pm. I'm flying out tomorrow at ten fifteen. It is a must win or we don't get to proceed. Assuming we are going to win, our next game is Thursday at noon. The whole thing ends on Sunday. I have an 11:00 pm flight pending, so I'll be home late, late, Sunday."

"So, do you think your guys are in a good position to win?" Elizabeth passed the pasta to Garrett.

"Well, the first team we are playing is undefeated, but our offense is really hot right now, so if our defense can just hold them in yardage, we should be OK."

Twirling linguini on her fork, Elizabeth asked, "Are the boys pumped?"

"Hell, they are just pumped to be going to Vegas."

Elizabeth laughed. "Well, you can't blame them. They are young and energetic."

Pouring more wine, Garrett asked, "So now what's your schedule look like? You seem to be going out of town a lot this year."

"Well, it's a presidential election next year. And we have lots of work to do." This excuse sounded hollow even to her.

"Let's see, so I am flying out Friday morning, we have a closed session Friday night, General Assembly opens Saturday morning, voting on Sunday morning, so I will also be home late Sunday. Oh, by the way, can you drop Sofie and Tink at the PetHotel on your way to the airport? They are expecting them."

"Yeah, sure," Garrett nodded as he finished off the French bread.

"Oh yes, and Kat called. She needs money for a boat trip her Biology Class is taking next week for some Marine Biology research project. Its' a couple hundred dollars, so I told her you'd call and give her your credit card number. Let's see, I guess that's it, I'll miss you." She grabbed his hand.

"I'll miss you too, babe. Maybe soon we can get away for a few days."

She smiled. "That sounds nice."

As Garrett left in the morning by taxi to the airport, sports bag in hand with two animal cages, Elizabeth took to the task of cleaning the house and packing for her trip. Shortly after 11:00 she received a phone call from the Republican Party Chairman.

"Elizabeth, I need you to get down here for an emergency session. We've got a whole block threatening to ask the Rules Committee to stop the vote. I want to call a meeting for tomorrow afternoon, as well as keeping the one on Friday. Can you get here? "

"Yeah, that should be OK. I'll let you know when I arrive."

"Thanks a million, Elizabeth." He sounded truly grateful.

"Sure, sure. No problem." She dialed Garrett's phone, knowing he was flying and couldn't answer. She left a voice mail message:

"Hi, babe. Listen, last minute change in plans. John Selznick phoned. Crisis already developing at the pre - convention, so I'm flying out today instead. You can reach me at the hotel or by cell. Love you."

"Three frickin' points. Guys come on, really? You traveled this far to choke and lose by three frickin' points? You were representing your state here."

"I expected a much better commitment from you guys. You played lazy and I think if each of you looks into your personal performance, we are all responsible. It was a cluster-fuck of mistakes. When we get back, two-a-days all week. Next Saturday needs to be way better than today." Garrett left the locker room hating being the ogre but he had to get the boys to understand that this late in the season every game mattered.

As he waited for his early flight home, he phoned Elizabeth, who did not answer. "Hey, babe, bad news. We lost right off the bat. Anyway, I am feeling horrible, so I am going home tonight, my flight leaves in about an hour. I'll probably sleep in tomorrow and then give you a call. Goodnight."

Raised voices, anger, pleading, too much coffee, noise, sweat, people, Elizabeth was done. She needed to retire to her room for the night and pick up the fight in the morning.

Waking late, Garrett spent a lazy day around the house, watching sports, munching on 'forbidden' snacks and beer. He took a long hot shower and tried to forget his team's terrible performance yesterday. "I need a vacation," he mumbled as he cleaned out the hair trap in the shower. He hung a picture Elizabeth had been bugging him to hang and decided to turn in early.

33
Chapter

One blast in the night; neighborhood dogs barking in alarm-the deed done. Lying in a fetal position, under the warm blankets, unaware. The figure in black turns and stealthily slips out the glass door with a guttural whisper - "Die."

Another long arduous day of wrangling and schmoozing, an executive dinner, plenty of after -dinner drinks, then back to the grind hammering out the deal before tomorrow morning's General Session where their platform would be presented. Shortly after one a.m., Elizabeth's phone rang, a number she didn't recognize.

"Hello?"

"Is this Elizabeth Wells?" the unfamiliar voice inquired.

"Yes, it is. Who's calling?" Elizabeth asked, a bit alarmed.

"Mrs. Wells, I am calling from Mount Sinai Hospital in Los Angeles, and I am sorry to inform you that there has been an accident."

"What kind of accident? Who?" she demanded.

"Mrs. Wells, will you be able to come to the hospital? Ma'am, your husband Garrett has been shot."

"Oh my God! Wha...no. Oh my God!" she grabbed her purse and ran out, speaking out loud to no one in particular. "I have to get to the airport." Driving her rental car as fast as she could with tears streaming down her face, a deep fear and pain in her stomach. Guilt, too much guilt. She shouted out loud "What the fuck happened!"

Rushing through the airport, she got a ticket on the next flight leaving in forty-five minutes. Sitting, anxiously waiting for the plane to take off, she debated whether she should have called the kids.

Finally arriving, she rushed into the hospital emergency doors. "Garrett Wells' room?" Frantically asking desk people, rushing down the nearest hallway, a tall man in a white coat and blue scrubs stepped in front of her, slowing her, holding her by the shoulders.

"Mrs. Wells? Mrs. Wells!"

She tried to push past him. "Please, Mrs. Wells."

She stopped dead in her tracks and looked him finally in the eye, noticing his glasses sitting a bit askew on his nose.

"Mrs. Wells, I am Dr. Bealer. I have been treating your husband for his injury. I am so sorry, Mrs. Wells, but we've spent over two hours working on him. Mr. Wells has succumbed to a single gunshot wound to his head. I'm sorry, ma'am. He's dead."

Without a word, Elizabeth fainted, overwhelmed by the news. Waking up in a hospital bed in what seemed like only a few minutes later, she saw the doctor again. "Oh my God, it's true, isn't it?"

"Mrs. Wells, we are going to give you a sedative that will help you," the doctor said gently touching her shoulder.

"Please, don't tell me the gunshot was self-inflicted." She knew that if it were it was because of her.

"Well, ma'am, there is an ongoing investigation, but as of this moment, the police don't believe it was. There are some detectives outside. They would like to ask you a few questions."

She laid her head back on the pillow, completely numb. The detectives had already been speaking to her before their next statement penetrated her head.

"We believe that an intruder broke into your home through the glass door leading into the master bedroom from the patio. There appears to be no forced entry, but the door was left open." She visualized the curtains blowing in the wind, in her now drug-induced stupor.

"We have canvassed the area. No one reports seeing anyone, but neighbors claim to have heard one gunshot."

"Mrs. Wells, did your husband have any enemies or anyone who would want to see him hurt or dead?"

She couldn't answer. She stared straight ahead, her mind slowly sinking into oblivion.

The doctor stepped up and said, "Gentlemen I know you need a statement from her, but she has been given a heavy sedative and she needs some rest."

In the morning, a barrage of questions started again. "Where were you last night, Mrs. Wells?" That was the last question she remembered being asked before she zoned out and thought about her children. Need to tell the kids.

34
Chapter

Funeral preparations, the service, the burial, had all been a whirlwind of activity done on autopilot. Elizabeth still could not grasp the idea that Garrett was gone.

Walking into the house for the wake after the funeral, many, many people, some she recognized, some she didn't, everyone wanting to say something to ease her pain. Didn't they know this type of pain would never go away? Trying to smile and be kind to those who loved her and her family, she really just wanted them all to leave, to let her grieve in her own way.

Karen, sensing Elizabeth was getting overwhelmed, swooped in and became her support both physically and emotionally until every-last guest left, except her crazy girls, who sat around her on the floor and sofas. Karen brought her a very large glass of wine.

"Do you want us to stay or go? Do you want to cry, scream, throw things? Tell us what you need," said Karen as the spokesman.

Taking a long drink of her wine, Elizabeth slowly lowered her glass. "I need you guys. Please don't leave me alone, not yet." Elizabeth looked exhausted.

"Of course, honey, Elizabeth, we are all right here for you," Corinna reassured her.

"I just can't believe he's gone." Elizabeth said in a detached, dreamlike way.

They all sank into silence for a few minutes. "So, have you gotten more information from the police?" asked Karen.

"Just that they believe it to be a random act of violence. They didn't take anything, Garrett didn't have any known enemies so that's where they are with it now. Where are my kids? I haven't seen them since I walked in."

"Oh, they are upstairs with their cousins and friends, trying to get through the day, much like we are down here," said Anna.

"Would you like me to get them?" Corinna volunteered.

"No-No, it's OK. I'll go up and talk with them later," knowing she really didn't have the words to say to them.

For the next three days her crazy girls became her sisters. They talked about everything under the sun, including her relationship with Peter, with her expressing nothing but guilt about it.

"Elizabeth, you didn't know this was going to happen. You were answering your needs with Peter. But you loved Garrett, Garrett knew it, we all knew it," Jessica reassured her. "Elizabeth, you had and have a right to be happy."

"But my happiness has come at a high price. Garrett died while I was having an affair with another man, I really don't know if I can live with myself."

"Garrett didn't even know, Elizabeth." Laura trying to help.

"Yeah, but I know-I'll always know." Staring off in the distance.

The next day she awoke to the smell of fresh bacon cooking and freshly brewed coffee. As she came down the stairs and into the kitchen, she found all of her friends busily making enough breakfast for an army.

"Good morning, sweetie. I went to your room earlier, but you weren't there. I figured you were in with the kids."

Karen rubbed her shoulder as she poured her a cup of coffee.

"Yeah, when I went up last night, we talked for a few hours, and none of us wanted to sleep alone so we all slept in Kat's bed."

"How are they doing with all this?" Anna asked.

"The best that can be expected, I guess. We are all on autopilot."

"I do want to have a private discussion with Kat. She knows about Peter but Julian does not."

"Julian does not what?" said her son, entering the kitchen scratching his head, hair unruly from sleep.

"Sleep in-you never sleep in! Want some coffee?" Elizabeth wanting to change the subject.

"Yes, thanks, Mom." She noted his eyes were puffy from crying. She felt instinctively protective, and hugged him tightly.

Karen said to Julian, also hugging him, "How are you doing, honey? Are you hanging in there? Anything we can do for you?"

"Can you bring my dad back?" he said with a quick retort.

"Julian!" Elizabeth understanding his pain, but wanted to keep him in check.

"No, he's right, Elizabeth. That's all we really want, isn't it?" Anna joined in soothingly. "Give it some time, Julian. It will become less raw." Julian shook his head and sipped his coffee.

"So, the girls and I were thinking, should we all hit the garden, get in touch with nature today?" said Laura overselling it a bit with a positive but barely believable enthusiasm.

"I have a better idea," Elizabeth spoke. "I'll sit in a lounge chair and watch you guys garden," with a small sideways smirk.

"Hey, honey, if that's what you want to do, you got it!"

"Mom, John's dad asked me if I wanted to go fishing

with him and Buddy this morning. I said yes. The quiet calm of the river may be just what I need today," Julian offered.

"I think that sounds like a great idea, son. Walt is such a good man. He knows you are hurting and he always knows the right thing to say, or not to say," Elizabeth replied, patting her son's hand.

The day was half over before Kat rolled out of bed. She had clearly been crying and her hair and makeup were disheveled. She came up to Elizabeth sitting in the lounge chair by the pool, putting her arms around her mother. "I love you, Mommy."

"Oh, sweetheart, I love you more than words can ever say. Come, sit on my lap." Kat curled up on her mother's lap as best she could. "There that's better. You've helped to brighten my day already."

"So, what are we going to do, Mom, I mean without Daddy?"

"Well, you and Julian are going to go back to school - soon. Your dad wanted nothing more than for you two to get a good education, so you have choices in your future."

"No, Mom. Who is going to stay with you?" Kat with a look of concern.

"Honey, I have my wonderful friends here, I have family, but most importantly I have to learn how to live without him. It's not going to be easy, but we all have to rejoin our lives at some point." As she spoke, tears trickled down hers and Kat's faces. "Promise me, Kat, when you get back to school you will continue to do as well as you have been. We can talk whenever you need to, but don't lose your focus."

Kat sniffled, wiping her nose on the sleeve of her robe. "I promise I will try to keep it up, but I am going to miss Daddy so much."

"Me, too," said Elizabeth, tucking Kat's head under her chin, again smelling the shampoo, of the little girl she was not so long ago.

"Your brother went fishing with Walt and Buddy. I think it'll be good for him. Have you thought about your day?"

"Yeah, Jenny is coming over. We are going to play video games all day, maybe go for a swim."

"OK, baby, whatever helps to get you through. Remember, time is the best healer." Elizabeth was trying to convey a strength to her children that she didn't even feel herself.

"I know, Mom. Please let me know if you need me or anything, OK?" looking at Elizabeth directly in the eye.

"I will, my angel. Thank you." Kat kissed Elizabeth's cheek and lumbered back into the house.

"Looking good, ladies. I think I want to hire you, all of you," Elizabeth said attempting a smile.

"No, not Karen. She has nooo green thumb! Everything she touches or looks at turns to dust." There was laughter from all.

After an hour more in the sun, Elizabeth called out, "Hey, girls, come here, all of you. You know what I want to do?"

"Tell us," Corinna said.

"I want to pop the hugest bowl of popcorn, pull out all the junk food in the cupboards, the kids' full sugar sodas, order pizza, and watch movies all day and night. Anyone with me?" Elizabeth needed the comfort of her friends.

"Hell, yes! Sign me up," said Laura, dusting herself off.

"God, Elizabeth, I've gained twenty pounds just listening to you," Anna laughed.

"Yes, but just think how wonderful you will feel after you've given in to it."

"Let's each pick a title of one of the best movies we have seen and force the others to watch it," Elizabeth said.

"Elizabeth, we are not watching Hocus Pocus again!" Corinna complained.

"No-No, it's not Halloween. I'll come up with a good one, I promise."

They settled around the large television in the den. "OK, OK, it's Elizabeth's house. She gets to choose first." Jessica always the diplomat.

"What will it be? Hmmm, I know. *'Shining Through'* with Michael Douglas and Melanie Griffith."

This was a spy movie and a love story set in wartime Germany. It had a harrowing plot but it was one that always made Elizabeth cry because ultimately it had a happy ending. As she chewed on her red licorice like she had never seen the movie, anxious about the upcoming battle scene, she reflected on how she did love Michael Douglas.

Surprisingly, when it was over the other girls said they loved it, too. Usually they made fun of her choices.

As Elizabeth was looking in the linen closet for piles of blankets, there was a knock at the door.

It was Kat's friend, Jenny. "Jenny, honey, thanks for coming to spend time with her. Anything that helps take her mind off her dad."

"Oh, no problem, Mrs. Wells. You know I love her like a sister. I wanna be there for her," Jenny with her sweet disposition.

"Thanks so much, sweetie. Just please promise to tell me if she needs anything from me and you girls are welcome to come join us for movies and junk food if you'd like."

"OK, I'll let her know. Thanks." Jenny turned and trotted up the stairs. Elizabeth returned to the gir ls.

"This night is missing WINE!" said Anna, jumping up.

"Oh, sweetheart, the pantry is full. Why don't you throw a few bottles in the fridge, and I think there might be one or two already chilling. Break 'em out!" Elizabeth instructed.

As the wine glasses were passed out, Elizabeth was really not in a partying mood and feared the wine might bring her down. She decided to sip very slowly. "Why are everyone's favorite movies the long ones?" she whined. "Just between *The Godfather* and *Star Wars* we've already spent five hours.

Whoever is next, make it a short one." Elizabeth laughed.

"Me, me," Jessica chimed in. "OK, this is one of my all-time favorite movies. It's about a disabled war veteran who eventually meets up with…"

"NO! That's not a good one," Karen said.

"What the hell, you guys got to pick your…" stopping midsentence, caught off guard by the stern, evil look on Karen's face.

"What, have you seen it?" Karen shot her another look and a sideways glance, as it simultaneously popped into Jessica's head that the vet was played by Peter Ballantyne. "Oh - oh yeah, that's kind of a long one."

"I know what you girls are trying to do. Thank you, but I'm fine. Watch whatever it is you wish," Elizabeth said.

Anna shook her head slightly toward Jessica. "Oh, I know. '*One Flew over the Cuckoo's Nest*', I love that movie."

"That sounds good," said Karen.

Half-way through, Elizabeth began to get very sleepy. She wanted to go to bed but dreaded sleeping alone. She knew she had to do it. Maybe it will be easier with the girls here, she thought.

"Well, ladies, this has been good, but I am so sleepy I think I am going to turn in, and I just want to thank you guys for all that you have done and are doing for me and the kids. You are all true friends. Thank you." A tear threatening in her eye.

"Anytime, sweetheart. Sleep well. Good night."

Elizabeth decided that she hadn't had that much wine and that she would take a sedative that the doctor had prescribed for her. She fell asleep in a haze, with her hand on Garrett's pillow.

This was day three. It was time to let the girls go home. After sleeping in late, she hugged Garrett's pillow to her, noting his scent had already begun to fade from it.

She allowed her mind to drift to Peter, for the first time since Garrett's death. She had sent him a brief email from the hospital to tell him of Garrett's passing. Although he had tried to reach her numerous times, she always let it go to voice mail. She wondered what all this meant for them. Would her guilt ever subside to let him in again? She still loved him but couldn't bring herself to acknowledge it.

When she came downstairs a bit before noon, Jessica and Corinna were standing in the kitchen talking.

"Hey, there she is. How'd you sleep? We thought we'd best not bother you. You need the rest."

Elizabeth smiled. "I do feel rested so that's something."

"Where are the others?"

"They piled into Laura's Range Rover and headed to the store. We're all going to have a nice brunch." Corinna sounding upbeat.

"You know, you guys are all so sweet, but you don't have to go to all the trouble,"

Elizabeth said, not wanting to take advantage of their generosity.

"Honey, we want to. It lets us feel that we are doing something." Jessica stroked Elizabeth's cheek.

"Oh, you guys are definitely doing something. I feel the love and the warmth. But I also owe it to you all to let you return to your lives, so after brunch, I want you all to re -enter society. I'll be fine and the kids are here for a few more days."

35
Chapter

Elizabeth awoke and knew this was the day. The second hardest day of her life. The day she had set aside to go through Garrett's things. What to keep, what to discard, what to pass on, deep inside knowing she wanted to keep it all. Having it around felt to her in some way he was not dead, that he still existed in her world. But friends, family, and colleagues had all urged her to push through her anguish and get it done. They said it was an important part of the grieving process.

She opened the doors to the large walk -in closet, looking at his side, the dark colors, running her fingers over the individual fabrics, recalling how he looked in each one. Tears welling up, she grabbed a handful of material and brought it to her nose, closing her eyes, taking in a deep breath of his scent that remained, and sank to the floor. "Garrett, I never deserved you."

She sat on the floor, separating clothes into piles, she then moved to the shoe boxes stacked on the top shelf of the closet. His favorite running shoes, his 'good' coaching shoes with the small metal cleats, his new leather 'business suit' shoes.

It was getting harder and harder for her. She needed a break. With everything she put into piles she felt herself losing a part of him. It was more than she could take.

Walking to the kitchen for a cup of tea, she stopped

short at the ottoman in front of the chair in the living room, remembering her 'crisis' cigarettes. Although she had given up smoking years before, she had a habit of keeping a pack in the ottoman for those days, once in a blue moon, when she couldn't find an outlet for her anxiety. Today was one of those days.

She laughed to herself. Garrett had always said smoking was a 'foul' habit.

Sitting in the window-seat in her bedroom smoking her cigarette and sipping her tea, she had never felt more alone. How would she get through the rest of her life without Garrett in it?

As she finally re-entered the closet, seeing more space freed up just made the emptiness she was feeling more tangible. She reached up for the next shoe box, much lighter than she expected. She opened it to find papers, a few various pictures, some of her and the kids, aged and sized so they seemed to have been carried in his wallet for a while. The family portrait by the Christmas tree, when the kids were still young, it had always been one of her favorite pictures. And another that made her blush. A boudoir beauty photo from a session that her crazy girls had talked her into for Garrett's birthday a few years back. She in a red teddy, stockings complete with garter belt, sexy smoldering look on her face and her big 'Texas' hair. She smiled as she remembered his reaction to the photos- desired effect.

Next, she came across ticket stubs from a boxing match he had gone to with his brother before Jack became ill with prostate cancer. At the bottom of the box was a 5x7 brown mailing envelope. It wasn't sealed, and it had no writing on it. She opened the flap and slid out its contents - two folded pieces of paper. She unfolded the first and felt that she recognized the writing, but she could not place it. It was not Garrett's. It began,

I am in love with Elizabeth. I know she is your wife and that she still loves you, but she is in love with me, too. I need her in my life .

The paper in her hand now trembling, her hand shot to her mouth. "No-No-No. Oh my God, Garrett. Oh, my God!" She continued reading.

I too am married so we do not plan to make disruptive changes to everyone's lives. Rather I wanted to let you know man to man that while the two of you may remain together, she is mine in every sense of the word and I ask you to honor and accept that. I do not plan on hiding my affections for her any longer. Peter Ballantyne .

She dropped the letter to the floor. Why would Peter do this, why? There was nothing to be gained, why? Feeling suddenly completely numb, she stared at the letter in disbelief. Finally remembering the other folded paper, she picked it up, slowly unfolding it and whispered, "God help me," this time recognizing Garrett's writing.

You have everything in the world, money, fame, good looks, a nice wife and kids. Why do you need to take my life as well? Don't you have enough? You are a son of a bitch and I will not let her go. She is my wife and she will stay that way. Leave her alone.

She dropped the letter, in full sobs, tears streaming down her face, and lay down in a fetal position. "Garrett, what have I done?"

Elizabeth woke hours later to the sound of Kat and Julian. "Mom, what happened? Are you OK?" As they knelt in front of her, she grabbed both of them, hugging them to her.

"Mom, what's going on?" Kat asked.

"Nothing, nothing. I love you both so very much."

"Aunt Meg said you were going through Dad's stuff today. We thought you might need some extra support," Kat said, brushing Elizabeth's hair out of her face.

"You're right, I do. Next to burying him, this is the hardest thing I have ever had to do." Grabbing the letters, she shoved them back in the envelope before the kids could see what they were.

"What's that?" Julian asked.

"Oh, just some of his paperwork. Julian, please go through that pile, there. They are some of your dad's clothes I think you should keep."

"Mommy," Kat said with a look of deep concern, "what can I do?"

"I could really use another cup of tea."

She knew with the kids here it would take all her effort to just get through the day without thinking or reacting to the letters. Later, after she and the kids shared the lasagna from the freezer that a kind neighbor had brought by after the funeral, the kids went up to their rooms. She finally re -read the letters, again consumed by uncontrolled tears and grief. Two thoughts came into her head for which she had no answers. Why had Garrett not actually sent the response letter, or had he? And the latter question created an instant queasiness in her stomach. Did Peter kill Garrett?

Spending a sleepness night contemplating these questions and reflecting on some of Peter's behavior, she phoned him. "Peter, I need to see you."

"Yes, love. Whatever you need I told you I am here for you. How are you holding up? What can I do?" genuine concern in his voice.

"Meet me here-in L.A.," She asked.

"OK, darling. I'll be on the next flight out."

She spent the rest of the day further researching Peter Ballantyne. Although she thought she had pored over much of the content she could find on the web when she first contacted him, as she began to type in narrower search parameters, she did come across things she had never seen. An old article about him being 'difficult' to work with. It explained that he was a perfectionist, and often demanded take after take on scenes until he was satisfied with them, making his cast -mates angry and resentful. And throwing tantrums and walking off sets and by other accounts being a down -right asshole. Others mentioned his having mellowed a bit over the years, but included a part of his history that included bouts of heavy drinking and womanizing.

Another article from a very respected British paper mentioned that while it was rumored that his was an open marriage, there had been several 'rows' between he and his wife, both verbal and physical, with police being called to their residence more than once. Elizabeth tried to rationalize that all of it; this information was old, over fifteen and twenty years. Although she had seen cracks in his personality, she had never seen anything in his behavior to this extent, or had she?

She did have to admit that he had said or done a few things out of character. She recalled him basically raping her, when he roughly took her anally, knowing he was hurting her. His insistence on knowing where she was and with whom all the time, also recalling the callous calls to his wife, and his physically grabbing Elizabeth herself in the tree incident at the after party. And then there was the discussion about the deep web-the deep web. She let that sink in. Had all of this been there all along? Had she just chosen to ignore it? Reflecting on what she was reading, she thought, how could I have missed all this? This is not how I see him at all. Usually sweet and gentle, a bit full of himself at times, but he's a celebrated actor.

They had arranged to meet in his hotel room. As soon as she came in he went to her wrapping his arms around her.

"I have been so worried about you. I tried to give you your space, but I really wanted to be here for you, with you."

Elizabeth pulled away from him, pacing in front of him.

"What is it Elizabeth?"

Looking into his eyes, deadly serious, she asked, "Did you kill my husband?"

"Did I what? Kill? I couldn't, wouldn 't ever do such a thing!" he was rocked by the question.

"This is not a game, Peter. My husband is dead. I know you contacted him." She showed him the letter.

Peter's face fell. After a few moments, he spoke. "I only contacted him and asked him to give you up for me," anger in his face. "I told you that I love you and I'll be goddamned if I was going to let another man keep you. You belong to me."

Elizabeth shouted, "So, it was you! You did this - Garrett is dead because of you!"

He shouted back, "No Elizabeth, I didn't kill anyone. I sent him a letter!"

"Peter, I love you and part of me always will, but I can't continue seeing you. I need time to grieve Garrett and to figure some stuff out."

His anger rose, "Oh, to figure out if I murdered your husband, Elizabeth?"

"Did you?" she shot him a hard look.

"Oh, go to hell!" he shouted. She gathered her handbag and the letter, leaving without a word.

36
Chapter

Into his second week of filming his current movie, Peter was sitting in Trader Vic's, Beverly Hills, drinking his third Manhattan and talking to himself. "I don't want to do this fucking picture. Why the hell did I let Barry talk me into this? Fucking agents are only out for themselves." A few more sips and he lit up a cigarette, a habit he had previously given up.

"Excuse me, sir, there is no smoking in here," the bartender tried politely.

"Do you know who the fuck I am? I smoke wherever and whenever the bloody hell I want to," re-lighting his already burning cigarette.

"I apologize, Mr. Ballantyne. Sir. You have had a bit much to drink. Is there someone I can call for you?"

"Someone you can call for me? You want to ring someone for me?" Peter getting louder, "You want to ring someone for me? Ring your mother for me!"

He threw down his lit cigarette, stood up and staggered to the door. He hopped in his car parked near the front door, heading to his agent's office determined to have it out with him about the stupid picture he had roped him into, completely unaware that it was past midnight and the doors to the large glamorous agent's office had been locked and deserted for hours already.

Blowing through one and then a second red light, luckily the traffic was lite at that time of night, but his indiscretions did not escape the patrol car sitting at the second light. With lights but no siren on, the patrol car pulled him over.

"Oh, what rubbish is this now?" as he opened his window.

"Sir, can you step out of the car, please?" The officer instructed.

"What for?" Peter said with disgust in his voice.

"Sir, please step out of the vehicle." The officer asked again as he shined his flashlight in Peter's face.

"No, I will not. Why have you pulled me over?" Slurring his words and making it clear to the officer he was drunk.

"On suspicion of DUI, sir." The officer opened Peter's car door.

"Oh, that's preposterous. Is it an autograph you want? A picture perhaps?" said Peter, ever the spoiled star.

Waking a few hours later in the drunk tank of the Beverly Hills jail, he was now aware and ready to be more cooperative.

"Sir, you blew a .18 blood alcohol when we brought you in. That is more than twice the legal limit to operate a motor vehicle in the State of California. Do you understand this statement?"

"I do," Peter growled.

"Sir, you are being placed under arrest for felony DUI." Once you are booked and processed we will place you back in the tank until you have completely sobered up." The booking officer doing things by the book.

"Call my agent-Barry Levy. He's in the book. Please, as soon as possible." Trying to sound humble.

"Yes, sir, we can do that for you." The young female officer shook her head.

Within the hour, Barry showed up. "This is Beverly Hills. You don't really think you are getting out of here unseen, do you, Peter? There are at least three television trucks out there already. This is a story. What the hell is going on with you, Peter? You've always kept this shit in check. I got a call from the Assistant Director on your film. She said you pitched a fit over some direction. I thought that your being difficult was in the past. What gives?"

"Sod off, Barry. I'm not in the mood for this right now. Take me home."

Five weeks had gone by since Elizabeth last spoke to Peter. He had called and left a few messages.

She knew he was in Los Angeles filming, but she didn't want to talk to him. It would just make things harder than they already were. She was mourning both he and Garrett. She had run out of questions, and answers.

Flipping on the kitchen television while waiting for her morning coffee to finish brewing, she heard, "Legendary British actor, Peter Ballantyne was arrested on DUI charges last night in Beverly Hills."

She sat immediately at the kitchen table. The reporter went on, "After resisting, and refusing a breathalyzer on scene, he was arrested and taken into custody."

The story was complete with pictures from the police dash camera as well his mugshot and video of him leaving the jail with his agent only an hour or so before.

"Peter, no. Oh God, what are you doing? I have too much shit to deal with right now. Peter, you are a big boy. You're on your own," Elizabeth said in her exhaustion.

The story played over and over on every news and entertainment channel. She finally had to turn it off.

He didn't attempt to call her over the next few weeks, for which she was glad.

She wanted to see him, but she was starting to understand he had issues, and a past. She had wanted to believe that for the most part that was behind him. She missed him.

Still she knew she was not ready. Garrett's death was still too fresh. She still had lingering questions. No, she would wait a while.

He called her the next day. Recognizing his number, she murmured "Not today, Peter. Not today."

37
Chapter

Another two weeks had passed since he last tried to contact her, and every day was getting harder for him. Drinking too much and chatting with Rex at Musso & Franks on Hollywood Boulevard, he said,

"Why are women such a pain in the ass I ask you, Rex, really? All you want to do is fucking love them, and they have a million issues why not. You know, mate? That bitch strung me along the whole time we were filming, fucking me, telling me she loved me, then 'poof', we are done filming and then it's 'I have to go home to my family.' What the hell is that all about? Do they think that men can't have feelings, man? I fucking loved her, the bitch."

"Now I have Elizabeth, I'm in love with her, Rex, her husband gets killed and now I must be the killer, she's convinced. Now I'll never see her again. Mate, I should stick with you. You got it all figured out, call girls and teenagers, no bullshit and drama!"

Rex, in his drunk stupor, "I don't know, man, I just don't know."

"I gotta get out of here, Rexy. Till we meet again." He stood up and slapped Rex on the back. "Take care of yourself, old man."

"Will do." Rex waved him off. Peter had been ducking the Paparazzi as they had been chasing him since the DUI.

Now, walking out of the bar, three different photographers were there waiting, one stepping in front of him.

Shortly after dinner, Elizabeth received a phone call.

"Hello?"

"Did you hear?" It was Karen, always the first one to know everything.

"Hear what?"

"About Peter."

Fearing the answer, she said, "What about Peter?"

"He's been arrested again, this time for assault. Turn on the TV."

"Only weeks after an arrest for DUI, legendary Actor Peter Ballantyne was arrested again tonight for assault outside Musso & Franks in Hollywood."

"Peter, why are you doing this?" Elizbeth in in exasperation. The station cut to a live report.

"Legendary Hollywood actor and longtime lothario Peter Ballantyne was arrested Wednesday night after punching a photographer outside L.A.'s famed celebrity hangout, Musso and Franks. Reportedly Ballantyne was intoxicated and became angry when a photographer stepped in front of him to snap a picture as he exited the bar. Ballantyne told him to 'get out of my way'. When the photographer continued to take photos, Ballantyne shoved his hand into the camera and punched the man knocking him to the ground. Ballantyne was overheard saying, 'I told you to get the fuck out of my face, you bastard' ". The station 'bleeping' out the offensive word, "but not before other photographs and videos captured the whole scene."

"Although Ballantyne left the restaurant, he was later placed under arrest at his hotel after being interviewed by police."

Elizabeth started to cry. As the reporter continued to talk, the station ran additional footage showing Peter punching the photographer, sending him tripping backward as his camera smashed to the ground, breaking off in pieces as Peter walked away.

Elizabeth could hear the photographer shouting after Peter, "You've screwed yourself this time, Ballantyne! You'll hear from my lawyer."

The pictures from other paparazzi showed the photographer, blood flowing from his lower lip, staining his teeth. Every single evening news program led with the same story, proclaiming "Legendary actor arrested for assault."

Then more pictures of him leaving jail with his agent, no comments, as he slipped into the passenger seat and the car drove away.

"I want you to tell me right now, what the hell is going on? You didn't even show up to the set today." Barry was fuming.

"Nothing, Barry, all right? Nothing is going on." Peter shouted, "I need a break! Get me a break from the film. I need a few weeks."

"Peter, if you do this they will assign a keeper to you when you get back. That's 24/7, Peter, and that's if insurance keeps you on." Barry being the 'super-agent' he got paid the big bucks for.

"Fine, whatever. I don't care. Just do it!" Peter with finality in his voice.

Elizabeth desperately wanted to call him, but as he was drunk and had just been released she thought it should wait until morning. But she still wasn't sure it was the right thing to do.

She continued watching the news programs as they began to dredge up his past so many years ago. But they also noted new rumors that he had been difficult on his new film, storming off in anger and threatening to pull out, people commenting that they thought that behavior was all in the past.

An unnamed friend was quoted in an interview as saying, "I'm surprised, because he's been able to pull himself together over the years as he's matured. It's quite unexpected at this point."

Elizabeth spent another sleepless night trying to figure her next move. Should she just walk away? But she knew through it all that she was still in love with him. She couldn't reconcile all that she knew, had been through. She was exhausted.

38
Chapter

When the sun came up, Elizabeth decided to walk downtown for a cup of Starbucks. The cool air helped her to clear her head. As she sat sipping her Cafe Americano, she recalled hearing during Garrett's wake from political friends that they had been successful in settling detractors' efforts to block her candidate's nomination. It felt like a hollow success as it just didn't matter right now, but she knew she needed to get back to her life. Sitting there she also decided, after her lunch with the girls today, she would call Peter to at least find out what was going on with him.

Only a few of the girls were free for lunch today, Elizabeth, Karen, Jessica, Anna, and Laura, but that was OK. They could really catch up with each other today. The first topic of discussion, and the reason they had decided to lunch today, was Jessica, and how she was taking Josh's latest Autism test.

"So, my son has had his third test to determine his position on the autism scale. In the two years since they discovered it, he has steadily gone higher on the scale, or less functioning for his age, so I am afraid of the results this time. I sense he has gotten worse, and I really don't know how to handle that, or him for that matter."

"Well, don't overthink it unless you have to. Wait for the results," Karen counseled.

Elizabeth asked, "If let's say it is worse, can they help you with him, the state or respite care?"

"I'm not sure. I plan to ask the doctor. His appointment is Tuesday. I'll definitely keeped you guys posted."

"Well, regardless honey, you know we are all here for you, Jess," Anna said, offering her support.

"Thanks, guys," Jessica said, averting her eyes.

"So, Karen, how goes the house selling?" Jessica said, changing the subject.

"Oh, our house has been on the market for nearly four months now. I am really beginning to worry that we are not going to sell it, or if we will end up taking a bath on the price."

"Why don't you just stay for a while until the market improves?" Elizabeth asked.

"With the kids gone we really just don't need all that space, and we have found a cute neighborhood about ten miles from here that we love. It's a little village and we can walk to everything, outdoor cafes and the like. We love it. The houses are smaller but really affordable. But this selling process has turned into a nightmare. You know, we even took out our furniture and are staging it. It looks fantastic. I just think it's still a buyer's market and there is too much choice," Karen said discouraged.

"Well, I'll keep my ears open for anyone buying," Elizabeth contributed.

"Me, too, girl," said Jessica.

"So, I did it", Laura said excitedly. "I registered and my first class in Human Psychology starts next month. I'm so excited. I haven't been a student in so many years, but I am so ready for the challenge."

"Oh, that's terrific. Good for you, Laura," said Karen with much enthusiasm.

"I'm proud of you, girlfriend," Elizabeth said grabbing her hand.

"I went through registration and orientation, and I was the oldest frickin' student. So many super young faces. I can't believe some of them are old enough to be in college. They even look so much younger than Kat and Julian." She glanced at Elizabeth, whose kids were the youngest.

"It's kind of scary though, some of them are wicked smart, but also scary because some of them are wicked dumb! I don't remember kids I was in college with before being so out of touch with adult issues, and just doorknob dumb. I feel bad for the future generations. It seems the smart ones are concentrating on only a few fields."

"Well, I'm so proud of you, Laura, for finally taking the leap. I know you have needed to do this for a while. That's the one thing about the kids leaving home. While there are so many negatives about missing them and the whole empty nest thing, it does allow us to revisit things we have wanted to do but kept putting off for our families. It's a bit freeing, isn't it?" Elizabeth observed.

"It's also frightening. Now I have so many hours to fill, I am not sure how," said Laura.

"Well, when you get into the full swing with the school thing, you'll be busy enough," offered Jessica.

Then the mood and talk turned somber, with Karen, the leader of the pack, broaching the subject. "Elizabeth, you know we all love you, right? But there has been something bothering us, and we feel we need to talk to you about it."

"OK, I'm listening," Elizabeth curious.

"We know you are in love with Peter, but Elizabeth, we are concerned. We know he has gotten into some trouble lately, and we were all talking about it the other night." Behind her back, Elizabeth noted.

"Anna recalled hearing some things about him a few years back, so she looked him up online. "

"There are many pictures and stories of him, firmly grasping his wife's arm in public, and rumors of verbal and possible physical abuse. It said he has had anger issues in the past, and with all this going on with him now, Elizabeth -is he treating you right? Has he ever gotten physical with you? Elizabeth, did he hurt Garrett?"

"Wow! That was a mouthful. Girls, first of all, thank you for your concern. I know you are asking because you care about me. And I, too, have had some of the same concerns. He has not been physical with me," choosing not to reveal anything, "and I have some questions and concern s about his behavior as well, in fact, I haven't spoken to him in quite a while because of it. I also had questions about his potential involvement in Garrett's death, but after talking with him, I have put most of those to rest, but we are meeting soon to discuss things again. So, know that I appreciate your love and concern for me. I think I will be OK, and that he was not involved, and we will be OK." A tear threatened to escape her eye.

Karen got up and hugged her. "OK, Elizabeth, OK, But, if you ever need anything from us, in any way, you know we are always here for you."

"Oh, you guys, I love you so much," she got up and they hugged as a group.

Lunch had been heavy today and left her feeling a bit down, but now she needed to call him. She bit her broken nail as the phone rang.

"Hello," he said in an uptight bothered way.

"Peter?"

"Elizabeth. Oh, darling, is that you? Thank you for calling. Elizabeth, I love you. I am so…"

She interrupted, "What the hell is going on with you, Peter? What are you doing? You are throwing away your career, your legacy, and for what?"

"Elizabeth, listen to me, please. I can't fucking get you out of my head. I don't want to be like this-this-I do things my way, people do what I want them to. You can't do this to me. You don't have my permission to do this to me. You're telling me, "I want you, I don't want you-Elizabeth, this is not a game, as you have said. I have feelings, too. I let someone I love walk out once. I am not doing it again."

"Elizabeth, listen to me, please," desperation in his voice. "My passport proves I was in Brussels. Please let me show it to you." She could tell he was crying. "I love you far too much to have done anything to hurt you so deeply. I would never- Elizabeth, I need you. Please, please come and see me at my hotel-please."

"Where are you staying?" she asked even though she was not yet certain she'd go.

"The Beverly Wilshire, 701."

"OK," she gave in without too much debate, "I'll be there in a couple of hours, but promise me in the meantime you are not going to do anything stupid!"

"I promise, Elizabeth. Thank you! I love you." She let that hang in the air without a response.

When she arrived at the hotel he immediately opened the door, pulled her to him and kissed her hard on the mouth.

"God, I thought I'd never see you again. I'm sorry about the letter to Garrett, but he wouldn't let you go, and I had to have you."

Elizabeth, although concerned she was so happy to see him too, it had been too long, she put her finger to his lips. "Shhhhh…." She kissed him long and lingering. She led him by the hand to the bedroom. They made love, sexual healing that they both needed with no words exchanged. Elizabeth, lying on his chest said, "Tell me about your past. I have heard some pretty disturbing things lately."

"Well, I used to be a real asshole, I admit it. I was a perfectionist when it came to my work, and many people took that as arrogance, so I did have issues with other actors and directors. I walked out on films on occasion when I felt I was in the right. I used to drink-a lot, with fellow actors, Rex and his lot. We had black-out weekends sometimes. We hung at the Playboy Mansion Grotto sometimes. I slept with a lot of different women, never anything serious. I did have an affair with a leading lady once that got a bit serious, but ended when filming ended. It hurt. A lot."

"What else? I was selfish about working and wasn't involved enough with raising my kids. There were long periods apart. Of course, that took a toll on my marriage as well. "

"I have had indiscretions I am not proud of, some I could be arrested for, but I like to think I have matured out of it. At least I thought I had until you told me you couldn't see me anymore. I lost it. I can't see myself getting over you."

"I started drinking again with Rex, who drinks like a fish, and it just got out of control. You saved me, Elizabeth, when you called. You saved me." Peter holding his gaze on her.

Silence hung in the air, as Elizabeth tried to digest his confessions. "Peter, have you ever hit Sarah?"

"Well, it's more like we've hit each other, not really punching or anything, just pushing and shoving during arguments, again something I am not proud of."

"Would you ever hit me?" she genuinely wanted to know.

"Never," a look of absolution on his face.

"You know you have been rough with me on a few occasions, and I don't like it." Not letting him off the hook.

"Love, I would never do anything to hurt you intentionally. I say things in anger, but never maliciously. "

"Elizabeth, I fully acknowledge I have been a terrible person in the past, hurt many people, but I am different now, especially different since I met you. Elizabeth, without you I have nothing."

"I love you, Peter, and I want to work this out, but I want to go very, very slow this time. I need space and time."

"Whatever you want Elizabeth, just don't ignore me anymore. I can't take it." Searching her eyes for forgiveness.

39
Chapter

They began talking more by phone, and emailing, texting more frequently, but not seeing each other as before. It felt right to Elizabeth. Even though they knew each other intimately, it gave them more chance to talk and to learn more about one another. This, she realized, should have been how it was from the start.

She was glad he was being open with her and admitting things she already knew to be true. It helped to re -build her trust in him. Had she accused him of something he didn't and never could do?

Had she been unfair, just because of circumstance? In three months, they had only seen each other once, in L.A. They had dinner and ended the evening in bed together, but parted knowing that this could put their relationship in high gear again, something she wasn't ready for.

Nearly six months had passed since Garrett's death, so when Julian called the family together to tell them he had proposed to Reagan and that they wanted to get married in two months before graduate school started, it was a lovely surprise but one that left them all thinking about Garrett and how they would be missing him for this special day.

"Two months. Why so soon? Oh, no, Julian - don't tell me…" Elizabeth said with concern.

"No, Mom, it's not like that. It just makes sense to do it before we both start graduate school, and we can get married persons housing on campus. I love her and she loves me and really there is no reason to wait. We'll just do a small, quick wedding."

Elizabeth put her hand up. "Wait-wait, no small and quick. Your father and I set aside two wedding funds, one for each of you." She looked at Kat. "We want to pay for the wedding. We'll sit down and go over the budget, but it should allow you a nice wedding with plenty of friends and family."

"Are you serious, Mom?" said Julian, clearly excited. "Wow, that's really nice. Thank you for thinking about us. I just wish Dad was here to celebrate, too."

"I know, honey, me, too." Elizabeth said feeling the weight of his absence.

Getting wrapped up with the wedding plans, and at Reagan's request being responsible for Julian's side of the family really had Elizabeth getting back into the thick of things. It helped her put her life back together.

Two weeks before the wedding, she decided she would ask Peter to join her for companionship, purely platonic for this event. When she mentioned it to Reagan and Julian, they were very excited. She had told them that she had met him in Europe and struck up a friendship. The kids were all very big fans of his work.

"That is the coolest thing ever, to have Peter Ballantyne at our wedding," said Julian with genuine excitement.

"Well, this is your special day, so I want his coming to be very low key, just another guest. Just let the invited guests be surprised if they recognize him." Elizabeth said earnestly.

"Are you sure about this, Elizabeth?" Peter said concerned but wanting to please her.

"Yes, Peter. I miss you something awful, and it's a special day for me. I'd love for you to be here."

"OK, you know I'm in Chicago filming, but I'll let them know today that I'll have to fly out for a few days, so they can shoot around me."

"This makes me really happy, Peter."

"Anything for you, love."

Helping the bride get ready in between having her own hair and make-up and nails done, being the mother of the groom was serious business. She was exhausted before the ceremony ever got started.

When the bride was ready, and Elizabeth and Peter made their way to their seats up front, two things crossed Elizabeth's mind- the whispers she heard as she walked by their guests, commenting on her looks, clothes etc., and of course, her escort.

Elizabeth had chosen a dress in lavender, with white mid-sized stiletto heels. Peter was in a beautifully -tailored light grey suit, expensive white shirt, new, dark grey suede shoes.

Finally, upon seeing Julian standing at the altar in his crisp black tuxedo, classic red bow tie, and cummerbund Elizabeth became overwhelmed by how much he looked like his father. It immediately brought a tear to her eye. He was so grown up, not a boy any longer. He was a man, a man ready to embark on the next chapter in his life, with a woman he loved at his side.

Elizabeth began a quick trip down memory lane. Julian in his first suit and tie for church, playing a tree in his first -grade play, trying to pull off Santa's beard at the mall. How fearful and sorry he was when he and a friend got caught throwing pebbles from a hill at the side of a freeway off -ramp and cracking the windshield of a vehicle, running home to Mom's arms in tears.

He hadn't known that the driver happened to be a friend of his father's, and therefore it was handled quite easily, but the lesson wasn't lost on him.

His dad showing him how to dance for his first Jr. High dance with the 'it' girl in school. Little League, high school football and basketball, it all came rushing back, causing

Elizabeth to dab at her eyes with the numerous tissues she had shoved in her sleeve.

Noting this, Peter leaned in and asked if she was OK. "Can I get you something, love?"

"No-I'll be fine. Thank you. Just having you here helps." She smiled and leaned into him.

Peter smiled. "There's no place I'd rather be today."

After the ceremony, with the reception in full -swing and the newlyweds leaving on their honeymoon, Elizabeth, Peter, and the crazy girls all adjourned to Elizabeth's house for more drinking. The crazy girls were ecstatic to meet Peter, and he charmed every last one of them.

Elizabeth was having such a good time, and too much wine, that eventually she sat on Peter's lap and leaned in for a long, luxurious kiss, which led to the girls cooing, and "Kiss, kiss," from Laura.

His deep voice broke the brief silence. "You know, I didn't get to dance with you at the reception, but I'd love to now."

Michael Buble played softly in the background as he stood and offered Elizabeth his hand. He immediately pulled her close to him, looking her deeply in the eyes, and then softly kissed her.

The girls let out hisses, and sighs of jealousy. He looked over and smiled at them.

"Oh, my God, you girls are like middle schoolers," Elizabeth admonished.

"Hey, we are living vicariously through you. Be quiet," said Karen.

She and Peter were good again and it felt right to Elizabeth. When the girls finally left at nearly two a.m., Elizabeth said to Peter, "I want you to stay with me, not in my bedroom. We'll stay in the guest bedroom."

Kat had already made plans after the reception that would go on for God knew how long, and she and Jenny were going to spend the night with Khloe. The house was theirs, but Elizabeth could not bring herself to sleep with Peter in the room she had shared with Garrett. They made love until dawn, and watched the sunrise from the bed.

"I know this has been a rough year for you, for us, but I want to remind you that I love you, truly, madly, and deeply, and that if anything ever happens to me Elizabeth, or to you, know this, for eternity, that I love you," he said. She knew what he was trying to say. Even though it was not something she even wanted to think about.

After a five-hour sleep, rising near eleven a.m., Peter spoke.

"How about I go for some fresh bagels, lox, and cream cheese, maybe some strawberries?"

"Oh, God, that sounds wonderful. I'm famished." She leaned to kiss him.

"I'm going to walk, see a bit of the town, and get some fresh air."

"Great idea. I'm going to jump in the shower." She kissed him again.

Just as she stepped out of the shower the phone rang. As she hurried to wrap a towel around her, still dripping wet, she tiptoed to the phone.

"Hello."

"Mom, hi, it's Julian." He sounded happy.

"Hi, Honey." Elizabeth was surprised that he was calling.

"Mom, we just wanted to call and tell you we love you and to thank you and Dad for giving us this wonderful wedding and this awesome honeymoon. We watched the sunrise over the water from our cabin; it was spectacular!"

"Oh, honey, I am so happy for you and proud. Reagan is a wonderful girl. I know Daddy thought so, too. He'd be proud, too, son. I love you both. Now get back to honeymooning and stop worrying about Mom."

"OK, Mom. We love you, too. Bye."

She sat on the bed, and tears came to her eyes, truly happy for her son's happiness.

While having their breakfast and gourmet coffee, Elizabeth said to Peter, "You know what we should do today?"

"What's that, love?" wiping cream cheese from her lip.

"On Sunday afternoons, the Griffith Park Observatory has an awesome planetarium show followed by an amazing laser light show set to music. We could take a hike on the trails, have a picnic lunch. What do you say?"

"I think that sounds fantastic. I hope you don't mind if I don a baseball cap and glasses."

"Not at all. I find you very sexy that way!" she winked at him.

"Wow, I never knew the Aurora Borealis was so beautiful! We should take a trip to see it for ourselves," Peter said in amazement after the shows. They walked around Griffith Park, sharing popcorn, visiting the carousel, watching the little kids have a ball, visiting the pony stable where the little ones got their first rides.

"I really miss my kids being that age. They were so much fun, and gave hugs and kisses so freely. They think you hung the moon at that age," Elizabeth said in a nostalgic mood.

"Me, too. It just seems like so long ago for me. It was hard to get used to not seeing them every day. That never really gets any easier. By the way. I'm old and I still think you hung the moon," smiling and pulling her in close to him.

"You are such the romantic."

"No, I'm British. Charm comes with the territory."

Elizabeth laughed. "You're looking tired, Peter. Are you getting enough rest? You work twice as much as a man half your age. You need to take breaks, Peter. It's catching up with you." She rested her hand on his chest.

"Are you implying Madam, that I look old?"

Grabbing his chin, she replied, "What, this face? This gorgeous face? Never!"

40
Chapter

Elizabeth had decided that her kitchen needed a makeover. No construction, just some sprucing up. In a t-shirt and with her jeans rolled up, she began by painting the walls a bright summery yellow. She decided she would leave the crown molding and baseboards a nice clean white.

She had already picked out some new wallpaper, a toile in light blue, but she was avoiding the task of hanging it fearing she really didn't know how to. She might have to enlist Kat's help when she came to visit next weekend. With the phone ringing, not sure whether to set the paint brush down or hold it, brushing the hair off her forehead, swiping it with paint, phone still ringing, she decided to just drop the brush in the paint can. Grabbing paper towels to wipe off her hands, she answered, "Hello?" She missed the call. "Oh, crap. Well, it'll go to voice mail."

She had forgotten all about the call as she showered and got ready for her political women's luncheon where the topic for the day was who would and wouldn't be working polling places and which ones tomorrow, Election Day.

The lunch was a treat today, prime rib with horseradish. She was in heaven. The speaker for the day, a local congressional candidate that the group had already been doing canvassing for, who had some funny anecdotes, and a serious message about get out the vote efforts.

After the lunch, she checked her phone messages, one sounding urgent from Peter. She hadn't seen him in nearly a month and a half.

"Elizabeth, its Peter. Listen, love, I need to see you. It's very important. Please call me."

She dialed his number. He answered on the first ring.

"Elizabeth, love, I need to see you in person. I'm flying out tomorrow. Can we meet at my hotel 'round seven?"

"Are you OK, Peter? What's up?" thinking he sounded too serious.

"I'll fill you in the day after tomorrow, but please meet me," he pressed.

"Sure. Of course, call me when you get in." She hung up a bit perplexed and curious. No sense worrying about it today. Tomorrow was Election Day, she had a lot to do.

After a long arduous year in getting their candidate nominated and getting out the vote, manning phone banks and canvassing since the primary victory, and with Elizabeth having her own heavy setbacks to heal from, it seemed, as though this night would never come.

In the large ballroom of the elegant hotel in Century City, with thousands of balloons safely being held above the main floor by netting ready to be dropped upon the prayed for outcome of victory for their candidate. Media outlets of all kinds staking out their places to interview the winners and losers, and to capture all the goings on.

This, the largest of the GOP parties, would be for numerous candidates statewide. So, many interviews were taking place asking for voter projections, and talking with candidates about what they thought their chances to be.

The Hors D'oeuvres and cocktails were all catered by the best caterers in town. People mingled and ate and drank, and when a new candidate made their way to the ballroom, the crowd would stop and applaud and cheer, the mood very optimistic and festive, flags everywhere, buttons and hats, a band playing.

This was the process of the transition of power in the U.S. in full swing, and it gave Elizabeth a feeling of pride about her involvement, and as she saw it, her duty as an American. By the end of the evening, she was victorious, happy, and exhausted.

In the morning, she was excited about meeting Peter later. He still fascinated and mesmerized her with his intellect and his body. Although she was a bit concerned about the tone of his call.

"Hello, love. Please come in." She stopped to kiss him lovingly. He kissed back but pulled away too soon.

"Listen, Elizabeth. Please sit. Let me get this out while I can. Please don't stop me," he said as his eyes focused on the floor.

Feeling for the sofa without looking for it, she sat on the edge, not taking her eyes off him.

"First, I need to say again, I'm sorry about the letter to Garrett." He put up his hand to direct her not to talk. "I just could not have him taking you away from me. He wouldn't listen to me about letting you go."

Oh, God, Elizabeth's heart sank. What was he going to say? She could feel the potential for her world to implode. He went on, "Didn't he know who I was ? The power I had over him? That I owned you and he no longer did? With him out of the picture, I knew I would be the only one you loved." Oh, God. He killed him! Elizabeth was in near panic.

"And that I would love you forever, but by out of the picture I meant if he let you go-for me. And that's all, Elizabeth." She was relieved with that statement, but where was he going with this?

"OK, Peter, so where do we go from here?"

"Elizabeth, listen." He sat, taking her hands in his. "I cannot offer you a future, even though I am so in love with you, and aside from the understanding between Sarah and me about staying together, I wish I had my life to give to you. But I have something I need to tell you. Elizabeth, darling…" She feared what was to come. Was he done with her? Was she losing him, too?

"Love, I am not well. I'm sick. I...am...dying." Fear gripped her immediately. Her brain screamed silently in her head. All she could do was look at him dumbfounded as he spoke again.

"My many years of smoking have caught up with me, love. I have lung cancer. I have had it for a few years, fighting it with chemotherapy and radiation."

Her mind drifted. So, this explained his occasional haggard look and tiredness and his love of hats.

He continued, "But there is nothing more they can do. It is spreading and not responding to treatment anymore." Squeezing Elizabeth's hand.

"No!" she shouted. "No, this can't be true. I love you. I need you," she said as she wrapped her arms around him, holding tight and weeping.

"I'm so sorry." He bowed his head. They held to each other, in silence for a long time. Then she pulled away quickly.

"Listen to me being selfish. How are you feeling? Does it hurt?" She touched his face as if checking for fever. "I wish I had been with you through this. Why, why have we not been through this together?"

He brushed away a single trickle of a tear threatening to run down her face. "We have," he said. "You have always been in my heart." Taking her hands in his again, he said, "I have loved you since the first night we spent in L.A., and I am so very sorry for what I couldn't give you. I never expected to fall in love with you." He went on, "Over the years I have had my share of affairs and one-night stands, but you, you Elizabeth, were different. You changed me in some way. I knew you cared, cared in a way that I haven't felt in a very long time." Boring his sincerity into her eyes .

Now the tears came down, streaming rivers, unstoppable.

With a lump in her throat she squeaked, "I'm not ready to lose you".

He gently wiped away her tears with his thumbs, lifting her chin so he could look deeply into her eyes again, holding back his own threatening tears. "Tonight, I am yours and you are mine. No one else in the world exists. Make love to me, Elizabeth."

They slowly and gently made love for hours, softest of touches, sweetest of kisses, slowly, rhythmically moving together, as he continued to wipe away her tears.

She knew he loved her. She could feel it in his touch, in his smile, in his eyes. Now she knew the story they were to tell. But she felt cheated. Cheated that she hadn't met him earlier in life. Perhaps they would be together in a permanent way.

She awoke the next morning to a solitary rose on her pillow, a note propped up against the lamp on the night table, addressed to 'Love'. It read simply,

I will always love you. Peter.

41
Chapter

She didn't get the chance to say goodbye and she knew she would never see him again. She was numb. She would grieve for them and their relationship, not comprehending how the two men she loved were being taken away from her.

She had physical symptoms her loss and grieving, not having an appetite for weeks, losing some noticeable weight, suffering bouts of nausea, and vomiting. Her body didn't know how to react to losing him.

As the weeks went by, she needed to know he was all right. No public announcements had ever been made about his ailing health. Throughout the time of their relationship he had given her his home phone number in case of an emergency or if she really needed him. She needed him now. At least a call to confirm he was still O.K.

After contemplating it for a few hours, she decided to make the call. Would talking to him relieve this pain and fear that had been burning in her chest? As she slowly dialed the number, taking a deep breath, she braced herself. The voice that said 'hello', was not his. It was his wife Sarah.

Elizabeth was taken by surprise. "Uh-um, hello. I- was hoping to speak with Peter."

"Who is this?" the wife inquired.

God what was she supposed to say? "A-a friend," she stumbled.

"I'm sorry, he's resting. Who did you say is calling?"

Taking a second too long to answer. "Oh, an old friend."

"Ahh, yes, the friend. Elizabeth, isn't it?" Sarah spoke with venom and an emphasis on the word friend. "You know I have known about you and Peter for a while now, hating you because I knew he was in love with you. I'm sure you got my email, but until last night, I didn't know for sure."

She continued, "He needed to lighten his conscience, and told me all about your relationship, and admitted as I suspected that he is in love with you. But Peter is dying and needs to be surrounded by his family now, me and our kids, and our grandkids." A catch in her voice. "Please leave it at that."

She hung up abruptly. The sting came with the words 'our family, our kids, and our grandkids,' of which Elizabeth was not and never would be a part. She thought to herself, how did I end up here? I just wanted a romance, and I ended up breaking too many hearts.

It was only three and a half weeks later, she heard it on the news, the death of the late, great Thespian and Academy Award Winning Actor Peter Ballantyne. She ran to the television, saw his picture behind the news anchor's head. Her legs buckled and she fell to the floor, grabbing her hair with both hands, knees up to her chest, rocking, rocking. No, Peter, no.

42
Chapter

Elizabeth had been summoned to the police station. They informed her they had some new information about Garrett and asked if she would come by to speak with them.

They had tried to keep her informed ever since the murder, but frankly they hadn't had anything new to tell her, the case had remained unsolved. So, when they phoned about new information, Elizabeth was anxious to meet with them.

"Mrs. Wells, have you ever had a relationship with the actor Peter Ballantyne?"

Stunned by the question, Elizabeth responded, "Why would you ask that?"

"Mrs. Wells, can you please answer the question?" the detective pressed on.

Feeling trapped but knowing she had to tell the truth, she replied, "Yes, I did."

"Well, in looking into your background, we gained access to some emails between you two, and we later confirmed it with Barry Levy, Mr. Ballantyne's Agent. He said the two of you had been seeing one another for quite some time."

"We have also been digging into Mr. Ballantyne's life and past to rule him out as a suspect in your husband's death as well. But we have recently been puzzled by something. We thought we had our answer when we had Interpol seize his computer at his home in Wales. It seems he had spent some time on the internet, looking into some rather dark thing s. Are you familiar with something called the 'black web'?"

"Yes, I was aware he knew about it. We spoke briefly about it. He said a friend mentioned it to him and he was curious about it." Elizabeth was now getting uncomfortable.

"Well, upon discovering these searches, including murder for hire, and later guns and ammunition, death, and flights to Los Angeles, a few curious things came up. One of the search dates accessed from his home desktop computer was when Mr. Ballantyne's passport puts him in Brussels. And even more curious there have been two search dates after Mr. Ballantyne's death, both on murder for hire. Would you have any thoughts about this, Mrs. Wells? I have to tell you we have been looking into your past ever since we discovered that you were in an intimate relationship with Ballantyne."

"Why? I had nothing to do with…"

The detective put up his hands, stopping her mid - sentence.

"We are not pursuing you as a suspect. We have verified your whereabouts, and we have looked into your ip address, your computer files, your record of travel and so on, and we are satisfied that you were not involved." This is what made us turn to Ballantyne. He had motive. But too many things are not adding up. It has led to more questions. "

"You stated ma'am that you went early to your political meeting because the chairman asked you to. We've verified this statement, and your travel, you also stated that Mr. Wells came home earlier than expected from his tournament. We've also verified that. This has led us to believe, Mrs. Wells, that you were the intended target, and if all had gone according to your original known plans, you, not Garrett, would have been home that night."

Elizabeth put her hand to her mouth with a gasp. "Someone wanted to kill me? Who? Why?" her head spinning now.

"Our focus now must turn to an obvious place. We will be interviewing Mrs. Ballantyne. Was she aware, as far as you know, of your relationship with her husband?"

Eliabeth nodded her head yes. "She had her suspicions, this is so twisted."

"Before we move on perhaps you can help us with something else." Why did that sound like a trap? Elizabeth thought.

"Yes, of course."

The detective reached for something beside his desk. "Some kids were recently playing in Rock Creek Park adjacent to your home and found this duffle bag thrown into the brush. Inside was one bullet casing, a ski mask, gloves and this." He reached into his desk drawer fetching a Ziploc -type bag with a label containing some typed information. "It had snagged and caught on the inside of one of the gloves, have you ever seen this before, Mrs. Wells?"

She asked, "May I?" indicating a desire to pick it up.

"Yes, just don't open it," the detective instructed.

Elizabeth was unable to catch her breath, not believing what she was seeing in front of her - the bracelet. The monogramed "M" bracelet that Peter had bought in Paris for Mackenzie's birthday. Feeling suddenly very weak, she dropped the bag onto the table.

"Mrs. Wells are you OK? Can I get you some water, coffee? Do you need a minute?" The seated detective asked.

The second detective, anxious, standing over her asked, "Mrs. Wells, do you recognize this jewelry?"

Her mind was racing but she didn't answer. "Mrs. Wells?"

Swallowing hard, she looked up at the anxious detective. "Yes. Yes, I do."

"Who does it belong to, Mrs. Wells?" he asked in a stern and level voice.

Hesitating in disbelief, in a near whisper she said, "Ballantyne, Mackenzie Ballantyne. Peter's daughter."

43
Chapter

After a request made by Mackenzie Ballantyne's lawyer, Elizabeth agreed to go to a jailhouse meeting with Mackenzie. As she walked into the police station, she asked for the lead detective on the case as she was instructed to do. She was led past various offices. She instantly recognized her, sitting in one of them, the blonde hair and deep creases on her face, Sarah Ballantyne. Who simply looked at her without expression.

She was led into the same detective's office that she had previously met with.

"Please Mrs. Wells, have a seat. As you know Ms. Ballantyne has confessed to the killing. We have further verified that it was she who conducted the computer searches in Wales. Also, through a BitCoin account that we had a tough time tracking down, we found that she purchased the murder weapon through the deep web. She was able to legitimately check it with her luggage on her flight to Los Angeles. "

These statements left Elizabeth wondering how all of this could have taken place without she or Peter, or anyone suspecting a thing.

The detective then led her down the hallway where she was met by a nicely-dressed man. "Hello, Mrs. Wells. I'm Anthony Stein, Ms. Ballantyne's attorney. Thank you for coming. You're here because my client is prepared to sign her confession, however, she said she would not execute it until she had a chance to speak with you face to face. You are not required to do this, Mrs. Wells. The choice is yours."

"No-No. I want to. I want to see her face to face. She took my husband's life."

Elizabeth was seated at a table in an interrogation room, with the standard issue police station coffee in hand, as Mackenzie, in cuffs and shackles, was led into the room, hair sweaty and sticking to her head and face, cheeks ruddy, looking as though she hadn't slept in days, and with an evil snarl on her face. She struggled to sit down, looking Elizabeth directly in the eyes without speaking.

Finally, Elizabeth asked, "Why?"

Mackenzie laughed. "Why-? Why?" She stood up and paced with obvious effort. "You," pointing with both index fingers through cuffed hands. "You were the one who broke my mother's heart. He had his dalliances over the years, the fucking bastard, but none affected him the way you did."

Elizabeth, confused, thinking she was here to talk about Garrett, listened.

"He loved you and that meant he couldn't go on loving my mother. Her heart was broken. She was paying the price. Did you know she wanted to take her own life?" Screaming, "SHE IS A CATHOLIC!! No, of course you didn't know, or care."

Mac continued with a low growl. "But I decided to take yours instead." Mac started to cry. "I never expected your husband to be the one who would die. For that I am sorry. He, like my mother, was an innocent pawn in the game you and my father were playing. I will forever be sorry I killed him, but I will always wish it was you!" she yelled. "He was my hero, my dad, my buddy, until he fucked my best friend, Caroline. How could he do that to me? He was my daddy, and he gave himself to my friend. How could he do that? Oh, I learned to live with it, but when I recognized the familiar pain he was causing my mother, no way was I going to let him get away with it again. I was going to make him hurt by taking away something he loved. It may not have worked out as I had planned, but at least I made you feel the pain of losing, the pain my mother was feeling, and that's good enough for me!"

Red-faced and now spitting, Mackenzie went on," I'll happily spend the rest of my life in this shit hole for making you pay." She turned away.

Elizabeth, silent, looked at the floor, finally raising her head.

"And what about your father?"

"Oh, I loved him, but I never have and never will forgive him. He could be the most selfish bastard around. He was loved and adored by his fans," turning back to look at Elizabeth, "who only saw what he wanted them to see. He always took whatever he wanted, and never had to pay the cost for it. With you dead-he would have finally paid. But God decided to end our misery and take him before I had the chance to kill you!" Mac was screaming now.

"Now you have nothing, Elizabeth, nothing. Garrett is gone, Peter is gone, you are nothing, and I hope you live the rest of your life in pain and regret, but most of all with the knowledge that all of this-ALL OF IT-is because of you, you fucking-bitch!"

44
Chapter

Ten days after the meeting at the jail Elizabeth received a small package she wasn't expecting. There was no return address. She had been trying to understand what had happened to her life. She had been deeply depressed for the weeks preceding, and now knowing her role in Garrett's death, losing Peter, she was lost, and she didn't know how to go on with her life without them in it. She was an empty shell. She hadn't eaten in days or showered in over a week. The house had remained unclean for weeks, as she kept dodging the 'crazy girls' requests to come over and take care of her, telling them she was fine. They, knowing that she wasn't exactly fine, but thought that they should give her some space.

With no energy or enthusiasm, Elizabeth opened the package. She recognized it instantly, a small card taped to it. The card read,

He wanted you to have this. Signed by Sarah Ballantyne.

As she peeled the note away, there was his ring. The one he always wore, even in his movies. That made her smile.

THE END